# STATUE of KU

by

## Tricia Stewart Shiu

Illustrations and Cover Photo
by Sydney Shiu

**STATUE Of KU**

by Tricia Stewart Shiu

Illustrations and Cover Photo by Sydney Shiu

Smashwords Edition

# Acknowledgments

I am deeply appreciative of the support and love given to me by my daughter Sydney, my husband Eric and my aunt/editor Rebecca Gummere as well as my friends and mentors: Gia Combs-Ramirez, William Hanrahan, Ingrid Lohneiss and Marcy Rydell. Thank you!

*"You can't stop something from being born."*

—Rebecca Gummere

# Table of Contents

CHAPTER I

# Blank Slate

Ritual: Invocation of Ku
Stone: Amethyst
Blend: Gem Elixir

*Create an altar outside. Use natural items when possible—a tree stump or a bed of moss makes an excellent altar, smooth stones to represent offerings to Ku. Spray gem elixir through ritual area and imagine it creating a protective light bubble around you and the altar. Before placing your stones on the altar, hold them in your palm and exhale your wishes and desires into each stone. Let each stone take on a specific wish or desire. Include as many as necessary. When finished, place offerings onto the altar.*

*Blessed Be.*

"Where are we now? All I see are clouds!" Moa's hands and face are pressed against the window of a luxurious private jet speeding toward Egypt. On one side of this ultra-sleek plane is an overstuffed banquette. Moa is seated on the opposite side in one of a long row of deep, plush, butter-soft leather captains' chairs that swivel. The cabin's fabric and wood colors are lush and verdant. Hand-hewn, richly stained wood lines the lower half of the plane's interior, and the upper walls and ceiling are covered in a warm sand cloth the color of the pyramids or dunes at sunset.

"Fruit, miss?" A beautiful flight attendant with glossy, black hair knotted in a low bun leans above Moa with a gilded, hand-painted tray arrayed with luscious island fruits—mango, pineapple, star fruit, papaya, and guava.

Moa chases a wiggly piece of mango around on the tray until the attendant sets it down and offers help by using some tongs, which hang on the arm of the tray. Her smooth skin and curious dark-brown eyes and high cheekbones are accentuated as she smiles. Then she gracefully places four pieces of mango on a white china plate with gold edging.

"I still haven't gotten over my recent transition to human form," Moa explains loudly to the attendant over the jet engines.

The flight attendant pulls back with a wary look and moves quickly to the back of the plane toward a large, curving staircase which leads up to a well-appointed kitchen. In front of the staircase is a large, round mahogany conference table with flat-screen televisions visible above the windows on either side of the comfy leather seats.

Moa looks over at Hillary, her best friend. "Didn't she understand what I meant?" She uses her fingers to capture the slippery mango then puts the entire dripping piece in her mouth.

Eighteen-year-old Hillary Hause is seated on the smooth, brown leather banquette opposite Moa's seat. She sniffs as she digs through her large, green leather purse, looking for a tissue. In her search she unearths a variety of artifacts in its cavernous depths: a scuffed and worn diary, an opalescent stone found in Honolulu's Thomas Square Park, a proprietary blend of essential oils and, finally, the elusive tissues. After blowing her nose, she opens the oil and anoints her forehead, chest, and wrists, tightly screws the cap back on, and throws the vial back in the purse. Then she chomps down on a tart slice of crisp, green apple she has plucked from the fruit tray.

"There aren't a lot of people like you here on Earth, Moa. In fact, you're the only person I know who was once an Ancient entity, lived on Earth for seven years in the mid-1500s, became an Ancient Gatekeeper, and then rematerialized into human form."

"Really? I thought there'd be at least one other." She grins at Hillary.

Her seven-year-old body probably would throw the average human off. To look at Moa, you'd never know that she carries with her an ancient wisdom. One that, despite her transition to the human form, remains intact. Her smooth, straight, dark-brown hair hits the middle of her back and she wears a tan, *kapa* cloth dress, handwoven by her mother during her first time on Earth. She has no shoes. So far, she hasn't needed them. She digs her toes into the soft, deep-pile, wool rug under her seat, pretending she is a Manx cat pawing at her pad. *Mmmm. Comfy.*

During her previous human state, Moa lived on the island of Honolulu, Hawaii with her mother, Lele—or as she called her, Maha — her father, Kapo, and two sisters, Amo and Re. A ship carrying strange men with long, dark beards and brown faces stormed the shores of their beautiful, peaceful village, first demanding food and drink, then grabbing anything of value from the family's dwelling. Kapo stubbornly refused and was killed along with Lele, Amo, and Re. It happened so quickly, there was no time to cry. The marauders ransacked their house and stole a beautiful black coral carving of Ku, the god of prosperity and production. Lele had been given the carving as payment for her diligent work on a *kapa* for a wealthy chief. She was widely revered as an expert weaver for her creations of elaborate ceremonial, gorgeous, uniquely printed kapa bark cloths from the *wauke* bush.

Each morning the family had said a prayer to Ku, a delicate six-inch-tall statue inlaid with precious pink coral. Moa's blood boiled, imagining her treasure in the filthy hands of such brutish men.

She had fled for her life into the brush and hid among the thorny gorse bush spines. Crying and weakened from grief and terror, she prayed the Huna prayer, asking for protection and salvation from her terrifying predicament. She began to breathe and to gather Mana—vital life energy—and send it to her highest self as she'd been taught to do by her Popo—grandmother—years before. The practice created a powerful bond with Popo, and when she passed—a mere month before the terrible invasion by the bearded men —Moa would feel Popo's spirit around her during her daily practice. Oh, how she missed her! As she sat amidst thorns and breathed the Mana, something extraordinary occurred—Grandmother's spirit came to her and lit up a small glowing hole in the earth, just large enough for Moa to enter. She did so in great haste and was enveloped in a protective, warming white light.

Popo said that Moa had entered the world of the Ancients and was safe. However, to continue to remain protected by the universal force, she had to agree to guide pre-selected humans through the portal to the Ancient world. Their own guides would meet them and take them to their destination of truth. Thus, she began her work as Gatekeeper for the Ancient Portal.

During her tenure as an Ancient Portal Gatekeeper, Moa had transitioned many souls from their bodies through the portal—generations, in fact. Her gift was to live between the worlds. And since her body did not die, but merely "transformed," she had existed in a vibration accessible only to those humans who chose to believe in and acknowledge her presence.

Moa's true home was in the Ancient world. She loved performing the essential duty of escorting souls from bodies to ensure their safe return to their destined spiritual repository. And her task was essential to the survival of the Hawaiian Islands because, although humans die, their souls must be transferred to the appropriate location. If not, and too many souls remain within the islands' energetic constructs, the Earth's energy will become unbalanced, causing natural disasters like volcanic eruptions and earthquakes. It is the human soul, which, upon transitioning to another state, balances and stabilizes the island energy.

The previous adventure with Hillary had culminated in a series of powerful events, which allowed Moa—with Hillary's help, of course—to restore balance to the Hawaiian Islands. However, the cost for saving the Islands had resulted in Moa becoming human, a state to which she was still adjusting.

The sleek private jet shoots past fluffy cumulous clouds and on toward Egypt. Moa settles back into her seat, puts her cheek against the soft leather, and closes her eyes.

I marvel at the smoothness of the sky, the warm light emanating from within the aircraft as it gently bounces along the crisp pockets of air. I remain just outside, beyond the small window near Moa's sweet face, where I savor the unique space between the outer world and Earth and prepare to approach the child.

It's funny that our journey would begin at the same place as did Hillary's and Moa's. So high up in the air, close to the thin veils that divide the ether from the real world. My reasons for being drawn to this plane are clear: I must go home. However, I cannot do so without the help of humans—and not just any humans, but specific ones with high-level spiritual skills and a unique knowledge of themselves and humanity. I need Moa and Hillary, and believe me, I am not used to needing anyone or anything. But more about me later.

To understand why Moa's and Hillary's help is so important to my journey home, you must understand their journeys here on Earth, and what has brought them to the present. Just one week ago, after completing high school, Hillary jetted off to Hawaii—her hypnotherapy "I'm Okay to Fly" recording was the only thing keeping her from climbing the walls of the fuselage, but much to her surprise, she made it just fine. The visit to see her sister, Molly, and her niece, seven-year-old Heidi, was beyond expectation, too. Her post-graduation gift vacation turned into an incredible adventure during which she and Moa met and became devoted friends.

Hillary expected to relax and enjoy her summer, lying on the beach and reconnecting with Molly and Heidi. Little did she know that she had agreed to help me save the Hawaiian Islands, which included battling Anuenue—pronounced Ah-Nooey-Nooey—who, although fully human, possess the remarkable gift of communicating with the Ancients. For all the incredible gifts the Anuenue possess, they are also formidable rivals.

Now that balance has been restored to the Ancient portal, and Moa is in human form, free to pursue her own desires, the first order of business is to find her mother's Statue of Ku. Balance is a tricky word. In Moa's case, balance included relinquishing her energetic body—and all the Ancient gifts that came with her energetic form—and to return to Earth to become fully mortal. Although all is not lost, she doesn't know it yet, but she will discover the wondrous gifts she can potentially embody here on Earth.

Molly, whose husband had died in a surfing accident a little more than a year ago, was skeptical as she watched Hillary develop rituals and practice her own version of energetic protection. Molly's motto was: "If I can't see it or touch it, it doesn't exist." However, she got a firsthand experience at just how powerful Hillary's work was when Moa showed up. Moa helped Molly understand there are some things that exist, even if we can't see them. And when Moa willingly and joyfully made the choice to take human form, Molly asked Moa to live with her and Heidi.

Despite her youth, Heidi exhibited much intuition and bravery on the first leg of her journey with Moa, and since they share the deep sorrow of what it is like to lose a parent, they both feel lucky to have each other. Hillary experienced Heidi's ability to connect with otherworldly entities when

Heidi delivered her first message from Moa. During a trip to Thomas Square Park, Hillary swiped a shiny stone from the base of one of the parks' many majestic banyan trees and slipped it into her purse. Heidi passed on the message that anything she removed from the Hawaiian Islands could cause her harm. Heidi even managed to deliver the news that one of the two boys who stole the artifacts from the Hawaiian Museum was indeed an Anuenue. A special pair of sunglasses had been surreptitiously delivered to Hillary by a thorny but helpful drugstore clerk and had proven to be invaluable at visually detecting Anuenue.

The rush of the plane's engines lulls Moa into a calm, sleepy state and she nestles down into the soft seat. Just as she drifts off, she feels the flight attendant gently place a blanket over her body.

"Thank you," she manages to mumble.

In her dream state, she stands in the brush near her island home and hears the familiar sound of her mother humming as she weaves. Lele doesn't see Moa at first, but she calls to her mother, "Maha!" and a rush of love courses through Moa's body as her mother, Lele, looks up and they run to embrace.

"My *keiki*." Lele softly breathes into Moa's hair, crystalline tears falling. "You must find the Statue of Ku."

"I will." Moa exhales a hiccup. "I miss you, Maha."

"Listen carefully. You must activate the statue in order to save Ku's soul."

"But, Maha, what do you mean by 'activate'? Also, he's a god. I thought gods existed at a higher frequency and therefore have moved beyond the soul level." Moa attempts to visually capture her mother's essence by memorizing the curve of her arm and the lines around her mouth. Who knows when she will see her again?

"It's true, however, that some gods were human at one time. Ku was one of them. When his physical life came to an end on Earth, his galactic family appealed to the Source Tribunal—the highest Light Collective in existence—to allow him to transcend to god status without his soul. The Source Tribunal allowed his status to continue on one condition: If his soul was not returned to his Earth connection—the statue—upon the death of his final blood descendant, he would relinquish his god status, and therefore Ku's descendants' life contracts would be deemed null and void. Anyone with a trace of Ku's DNA will instantly perish. Because I am a descendant, I was given the task of locating the soul and placing it into the statue."

"What does the 'soul' look like?" Moa says, exasperated and desperate with the task that her mother has laid out for her.

"I searched my entire Earth life for Ku's soul, but the only clue I found is that it is said to sparkle like water, but is not of the sea. You must succeed at retrieving the Statue of Ku, dear one. If you fail, not only will Ku and his sole blood descendant perish, but Ku's distant descendants—and we are among them—will cease to exist."

A tear runs down Moa's cheek and her mother squeezes her lovely child in tighter. Moa inhales Lele's light, her memory, her spirit.

Lele holds Moa close but her energy begins to fade. Moa does her best to snuggle into the embrace, but feels the softness of her mother's form dissolve around her trembling arms.

"You are such a clever child. I know you will succeed." Moa's hands can no longer feel Lele's misty but energetic body. Her mother is now a filmy memory.

Up to this point, Moa had always thought she knew where her family was. They had gone into the Light. So she asks, "Maha, where are you? Where is everyone else?"

Lele's last words before she completely disappears are, "Your sisters and father went into the Light, but I stayed behind to retrieve the statue. I am stuck in another dimensional universe—light years from here—and am here now because you are so close to retrieving the Statue of Ku. When you do so, you will free me and I will join the rest of our family in the Light."

"Wait…Maha." Moa calls after, but Lele is gone.

Moa awakens to the smooth white noise of the plane's engines. The suede beneath her face is moist with tears, as are her cheeks and chin. She makes herself get up and walk around. The man called the Guardian dozes peacefully. Moa is finally able to get a good look at him and can find no trace of his gruff demeanor as he gently snores. His thick, black hair is carefully smoothed back with gel, his clean, brown skin shows only a few wrinkles around his eyes, and his mouth is relaxed.

This man is the Guardian of two teenaged boys who, although not related to Emel Shanheer, the blood descendant of King Tutankhamen, remain loyal to the king's wishes. The young boys call themselves the Rindodala Sect, a group who consider themselves Egyptian Robin Hoods. They were arrested in Honolulu in connection with the thefts of three priceless museum pieces taken from the Honolulu Museum of Art. One of these pieces was Moa's mother's Statue of Ku. After accepting full responsibility for the thefts, the Guardian claimed diplomatic immunity for the teens, so Hawaiian officials had no choice but to permit them to take the items back to Cairo. The Guardian and the teens insisted that the items were all part of the royal family's collection.

Moa had dragged Hillary with her as she jumped into the Guardian's limousine departing for the airport, and the Guardian agreed to allow her and Hillary to come along on the trip and stay and dine at the palace on one condition: Moa must prove that the Statue of Ku belonged to Moa's mother. Otherwise, not only would Moa and Hillary owe a lot of money, they could be imprisoned for slander. If that wasn't frustrating enough, the Guardian allowed the teens in his charge to leave on a separate aircraft, taking her mother's statue with them! Moa's plane is about two hours behind the teens' aircraft, which carries the Statue of Ku, but she is determined to locate it despite the increased lag time.

Even though her telepathic gifts are gone, Moa understands intuitively that the Guardian is doing a job and that his protective nature and sharp exterior are not all there is to him. Still, his name and true intentions remain a mystery.

Hillary is asleep, snuggled on the banquette with her knees curled close to her body. She shifts her feet under her soft cotton blanket covering. Moa contemplates squeezing herself next to Hillary, but decides against it. Both of them have had very little sleep during the last week and she doesn't have the heart to wake her friend. The flight attendant is reading, and judging by her wary response earlier in the flight, is not open to conversation.

Moa crawls back into her seat, faces the window, and wishes herself home—wherever that is. Her eyes again begin to leak tiny tears, which, because she is lying on one side, run across the bridge of her nose and down her right cheek.

"Would you like a treat?" Moa feels a hand on her shoulder and turns to see the Guardian warmly smiling down at her.

"Um, sure." She sniffs and wipes the tears with the back of her hand as he gives her a beautiful, fabric-covered box. Inside is a shimmering marzipan scarab.

"Please, call me Paul."

"Thank you, Paul." Moa picks the greenish opalescent beetle up and holds it in the light. Its vermillion wings sparkle.

"Legend says that if one eats the scarab, luck and good fortune will surely come."

"The Statue of Ku is my mother's," she says quietly.

"I hope that is true." Paul says solemnly, "Remember our deal?"

Moa nods, thinking of all the money she might owe— how could she possibly pay off such a debt? Worse, what would the inside of an Egyptian jail cell be like? One last hiccup escapes from her tiny throat with a quiet sound. *Eep.*

"For now," Paul says kindly, "eat the scarab. And may luck be on your side. Also, on your inside." He lets out a huge, warm laugh.

# CHAPTER II
# Ku

Ritual: Heart of Ku
Stone: Rose Quartz
Blend: Full Moon Elixir

---

*The morning of the full moon, find a smooth, medium-sized stone and bathe it in sea salt and water. Dry it thoroughly, set it onto a patch of earth, and let it to sit for the day. As the full moon rises that same evening, place your hands on the stone—which is now filled with the beautifully grounding Earth energy, and ask to release all fears, worries, and blocks contained within your body, mind, and spirit into the stone. Feel the heaviness leave your body and allow it to be drawn into the stone. Now, ask to be filled with the grounding, centering energy of Ku.*

*Know that it is so.*

*Blessed Be.*

Hillary's thoughts are filled with her sister, Molly. When she was six years old, Molly, sixteen, was in charge of teaching Hillary the proper way to do household chores. Molly would stand and watch as Hillary tried to carefully wash the dishes without chipping a plate. If Hillary so much as clinked a plate against the sink, Molly would wince, which set Hillary on edge. In Hillary's opinion, Molly made everything a chore—did she prepare the water? Don't use too much soap and God forbid if she slipped and dropped a glass into the soapy water. "Watch out" should be Molly's middle name. After all, she and Moa had left Hawaii on a whim—something that Molly's structured, concrete mind has a hard time embracing. Hillary smiles as she pictures Molly's likely reaction. Moa and Hillary's rash decision—Hillary is sure—has gotten under Molly's skin. And for some reason there is something deliciously thrilling about getting under Molly's skin.

As she and Moa sped toward the airport, Hillary attempted to explain the situation to her sister on her cell phone, but didn't get far before Molly started in with a barrage of questions.

Always the self-appointed voice of reason, Molly was wildly unhappy about their departure. "You don't have much money. Where will you stay? How will you eat? For heaven's sake, she doesn't even have shoes!"

"It's okay, Mol." Hillary tried to keep her tone even. "They've assured us that we will have a place to stay when we land." Of course, she left out the fact that the Guardian's agreement is conditional, and that if Hillary and Moa fail they will owe the royal family the price of a round-trip private jet trip, lodging, meals, and whatever else comes their way.

Hillary knew Molly could not afford to come to Egypt, so when the call was cut off—by accident, of course—Hillary opted not to call back. For all her annoying, nitpicking ways, though, Molly had made several good points. Hillary and Moa had no money, no lodging, and, aside from getting on a plane to Egypt, no solid plan.

The plane jolts, then shudders as it hits the dry desert runway. A colorful flock of Safi Egyptian Swift pigeons scatter, and the jet taxis up to a large cinder-block private airport. Five armed, uniformed royal police wait in the dry, shimmering heat as plainly clothed servants wheel a gold-carpeted rolling staircase up to the plane and lock it in place.

"What's happening?" Hillary asks quickly.

"Don't worry." The Guardian stretches and pulls a freshly laundered coat out of the back closet. "It's just the royal police. They check identification upon entering our country. A simple driver's license, birth certificate, or passport is sufficient for private visitors and guests of the royal family."

*Moa has no birth certificate!* How could she have missed this incredibly obvious detail? Hillary nervously watches the Guardian as he busies himself with gathering his belongings. Grabbing her purse, she scoots into the seat beside her beloved and quirky travel companion.

The officers noiselessly board the plane. Four of them stand stiffly at the front, their AK45s hung by straps across their broad shoulders. A beautiful Monarch butterfly follows them in and flits around their heads before wending its way through the cabin, the kitchen, the cockpit, and eventually toward Hillary and Moa. None of the officers notice it, but Moa keeps her eyes fixed on the butterfly's orange and black wings. It's as if the creature is doing a thorough inspection of the vessel.

"I've got a driver's license," Hillary whispers intensely, "But, Moa, you don't have any identification. No passport. Nothing at all!"

A particularly intense-looking officer approaches the Guardian.

"Don't worry." Moa leans back and smiles. "It's under control. The Monarch butterfly means everything will be okay."

"Moa, I don't think you understand. People here on Earth don't take kindly to people who skirt the system. Those guns are real!"

The Guardian and the officers noiselessly acknowledge each other officially by bowing and nodding. Then an unusually scruffy-looking officer turns his gaze toward Hillary and Moa. His black hair has been combed and gelled, but four unruly cowlicks send tufts of hair springing outward. His beard is carefully trimmed, but the color is patchy with splotches of red and gold within the black hair.

"How can someone who tries so hard to look neat and tidy look so messy?" Moa whispers and nudges Hillary in the ribs.

"Moa!" Hillary's body stiffens as the unkempt officer approaches.

"Remember, you can see me but they can't." Moa gently pats Hillary's arm and says confidently. "It's okay."

Hillary rolls her eyes, emits an exasperated sigh, and looks out the window.

The tallest of the officers pushes by the unkempt one, gives a wink to the flight attendant as he moves past, and addresses Hillary. "Identification please."

His haughty air unnerves Hillary. Suddenly, this whim of a trip seems more ill–advised—with every second she must bear the officer's unsettling focus. Her stomach tightens as she carefully digs through her messy, green, leather hobo bag to produce her driver's license.

"Here you go." Then she quickly adds, "I know…bad picture…"

Moa's energy work is almost as natural as breathing. A thought becomes an intention, which makes it reality. She calmly invokes an energetic cloak—as she's done thousands of times before—and smiles as the snarky officer hands Hillary's license back. It's so fun toying with mortals.

"And what have we here?" The snarling royal police officer adjusts his large gun and takes two steps in Moa's direction. "Identification please." He spits the "p."

Moa remains motionless, then slowly turns her head to look behind her. Surely there is another person he is addressing.

The officer leans down toward Moa until his face is inches from hers, "I do not like to repeat myself." The smile fades and is replaced by a gritty snarl.

"Hello, sir. There is no need to get upset. I merely was attempting to use a cloaking field which failed because I am now human." *Gulp.*

Hillary jumps to Moa's rescue. "After all," she lets out a nervous laugh, "To err is human."

"Yes, yes." Moa gives a genuine smile. "And to forgive is divine."

The officer's visage morphs into a disinterested stare as he turns to the three men behind him. "Take them away."

He doesn't even look back as he turns on his heel, steps down the aisle, and descends the stairs.

"But, the butterfly!" Moa looks incredulous as an officer wraps his thickly calloused hands around her slim bicep and lifts her out of her seat. "I was sure it meant we were safe."

Hillary barely has time to sling her purse over her shoulder as another man handcuffs both her wrists in front of her body, "Moa. Sometimes a butterfly is just a butterfly."

Now, on to my story…

In my family, healing abilities skip a generation, and since I was the last male born to my parents and none of my brothers was the lucky recipient of these ancient gifts, my parents held their breath after I was born. Would I carry this preternatural gene? Or would I be doomed to walk this Earth as a mere mortal?

When I was six months old, the village Shaman held a ritual that had been passed down for more generations than could be counted. He asked the gods to facilitate a demonstration of my healing abilities, in the form of healing the sick. The Shaman brought his prized pet lynx, which had been injured by a hyena protecting the Shaman when he was on walkabout. All in attendance held their breath to see if I would be worthy of being called "Healer."

My father placed me in a ceremonial cradle made of woven green twigs and lined with soft grass. Then he sat close to the cradle, lest anything happen. One can never be too careful with a hurt animal, even if it was tame. The lynx had to be carried, by the Shaman, to a mat in the middle of the sacred circle. Its limp body shuddered with labored breathing and the Shaman removed a clump of healing *ponoka* leaves to reveal an infected wound on the suffering cat's hind leg.

The Shaman incanted the ancient words to bring protection and miracles and silently knelt beside his beloved lynx, which was immobile with pain. A hush fell as the group waited for the healing to occur, but instead the cat jerked forward, extending its front sinewy leg with claws shooting toward my tiny body. Quick as a flash, my father snatched me from harm and the Shaman leapt to retrieve the lynx by the neck.

The cat had sliced my soft baby flesh with his razor-like claws and the group let out an audible gasp as the wound sparkled with light and was instantly healed, leaving a scar bearing the mark of the cat's claws—three parallel lines on my right hip. In the same instant, the lynx's infection was cleared and the skin around its wound became pink and newly healed.

As the group cheered and clamored to catch a glimpse of their new star, the Shaman took me in his arms, held me up as in offering to the blazing noonday sun and declared, "Blessed Light. He is 'the Healer.'"

My parents proudly joined my side as he proclaimed, "This child will forevermore be called 'Ku Re,' the divine luminous Light from within, and will bring wealth and healing to all he encounters. Subsequent generations will bear the mark of the chosen one. I anoint you the Prince of Light, Lord of Healing, Blessed god, Ku."

I became simply, "Ku."

At the time of my birth, the land around my people was changing rapidly. Our once verdant, lush forests were drying up. This lack of water caused desperation among animals as well as people. Our village was once known for its goat's milk. People would walk for miles to buy a pail to nourish their family. However, as the climate changed and our village's resources diminished, the people of our village focused on survival.

At a very young age, I used my healing abilities to restore health to people and animals. It seemed that, at least for a while, I brought hope back to the village. Before the age of five, I revived three goats, a male tribe elder, and a baby who had accidentally fallen, hit her head on a rock, and stopped breathing.

People began to show up and ask my parents for help, offering food and water in exchange for my healing touch.

Not only were my gifts a source of pride with my family, they became a source of sustenance. My siblings were jealous and argued about why they had to work hard when I was perfectly capable of doing chores; however, my parents told them that I needed time to cultivate my gifts. Although I couldn't change the plight of the continually changing climate, I could help my family stay alive.

Since my healing abilities had always been with me, accessing them came naturally. I would sit on a rock facing the morning sun as it rose over the purple and orange rock formations and breathe in the beautiful dawn. As I did so, I would close my eyes and meditate deeply. During these meditations, I would often go on "journeys," during which I would meet all manner of guides and angels who would teach me more about my gifts. What joy my healing abilities brought me!

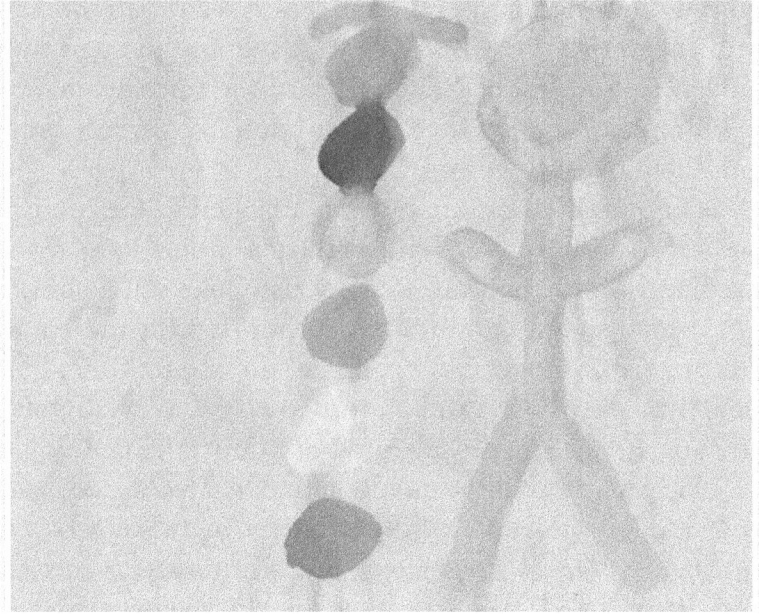

One particularly warm morning when I was seven years old, I hadn't slept well, having dreamt that someone needed my help. I was wakened by the sound of a woman calling out. My investigation led me to the meditation rock but no one was there. I could have sworn I heard a woman's voice calling, "Help me..."

I was at my normal meditation spot and it was dawn, so I decided to go through my morning ritual. As the sun began to light up the sky, I descended deeper and deeper into my meditation, and I found myself somewhere new—standing in front of a large stone temple with a pointed, tiered roof and carved statues on the outside. I'd never seen such a magnificent structure, and I decided to explore the interior.

Then I heard it again, a woman crying out, "I need help!"

Cautiously, I walked between two large columns and entered the cool, shady entry hall. Frescos covered the walls and I marveled at the intricately carved and painted staircase leading downward. Then I heard the voice again.

"Oh, please I need help." It sounded like it was coming from the base of the stairs.

As I got to the bottom, my eyes adjusted to the dimly lit corridor in front of me. Torches flickered on a long, stone-paved and walled hallway. I could just make out a glowing light, which shone from underneath a door at the end of the corridor. No one said my name, no one told me, but I knew this was where I was supposed to go. When I got to the door, I heard a rustling and faint murmuring. A jolt of fear made me stop for just a moment. *Did I really need to help this woman? I could easily end my meditation and allow her to find her own way through her troubles.* But, as quickly as the fear came it departed, and I pushed the thick, heavy, ancient door open.

# CHAPTER III
# Gratitude

## Ritual: Healing the Mind
## Stone: Carnelian
## Blend: Thought Venom Elixir

---

*Before you go to sleep, place a piece of paper, a pen, and an empty*
*cup next to your bed. Upon waking in the morning, before you*
*rise, catch your first thought. Write that thought down, fold it,*
*and place the paper into the cup next to your bed. Perform your*
*thought collecting for four more mornings. On the fifth morning,*
*place your papers in an urn or a fire-safe container and light*
*them with a match. As your first thoughts burn, say the following,*
*"I believe in the power of the mind, the body, and the spirit. The*
*mind is merely one piece of the whole. I am whole."*

*Blessed Be.*

"**L**ook, we're very sorry we caused a problem." Hillary pleads with an efficient–looking, stony-faced, male officer who sits behind a desk. She and Moa stand in front of his neatly organized desk, pleading their case. "My cell phone won't work here. If you could just let me use your phone, I could call my sister, in Hawaii, and I'm sure we can get this all worked out."

Without a word, the officer motions for them to sit in a row of newly painted metal chairs lining the wall and returns to his work at a computer.

The truth is Hillary's not sure what she would say to Molly even if she could call. Moa has no identification because she just became human yesterday. But given the unusual nature of these past weeks, it does not surprise her in the least that she half-believes she and Moa will find a way out of the mess.

Hillary takes the opportunity to look around the office. Piles of musty books are stacked atop army-green metal file cabinets. The whole place has a layer of soot or dirt. Whichever it is, Hillary keeps her hands to herself. You'd think royalty would be a little more conscientious about their housekeeping—even if it is a dusty little box of a building somewhere between the royal airport and who knows where.

The officer sits amidst this clutterter on a pristine island of organization. His crisply creased pants barely wrinkle at his knees and elbows, thanks to his pert posture, which keeps his clothing neat as a pin. Stiff and sharp, this man says nothing, but his body speaks volumes—*Stay in line or else...*

Oblivious to the unspoken warning, Moa hops up on a chair and dangles her legs above the floor. "We just came here to get the Statue of Ku. Is there any way you can let us go if we promise to return with proof that the statue is rightfully mine?"

The officer's bemused look says it all.

Hillary takes one more shot at convincing the officer, now engrossed in a thick book with a picture of a Spanish mission on the cover. "Um...excuse me..."

Her polite query is met with a withering glare but she continues. "I see you like Spanish architecture. Are you, by any chance, interested in the legend of Señorita Matilde Regnetto?"

He puts down his treasured book and although he still reveals no smile, his stern look opens slightly to a more neutral one.

Hillary believes she has the tip of one toe in the slamming door that separates her and Moa from incarceration, so she seizes the opportunity. "Matilde was only fifteen when she lost her life in a fire while she was trying to save her little sister."

The officer nods slightly and Hillary continues. "Her father abandoned the family of six children and her mother died, leaving them to fend for themselves..."

"Hillary lived in Los Tardos, California, where there is a famous mission. That's how she knows so much about Matilde," Moa helpfully interjects.

Hillary does not need help. "Matilde and her siblings ended up in the mission when the kind nuns took them in." She can feel that the officer is, ever so slightly, gaining interest. "The nuns of the Los Tardos mission commissioned a painting and plaque for the mission's vestibule."

"Hillary has seen it," Moa adds excitedly. She jumps to her feet and exclaims, "In fact she has seen Matilde. Tell him, Hillary."

The officer grabs a two-way radio and sharply mumbles something in it, his eyes still glued on the two. A jolt goes through Hillary as she feels all of her hard work at warming up the officer drain away.

Shaking his head and muttering to himself, the officer returns to his work.

Oblivious to any danger she might bring to she and Hillary with her words, Moa turns to Hillary and says with a shrug. "I guess he's of a more scientific mind-set."

Hillary, however, has been keenly aware of the officer's distaste for them and swallows hard as she follows his hand from his keyboard as it slides down to the gun holster on his thigh. He gives the gun a pat and then, once more, returns to his work.

"Moa," Hillary puts her lips close to Moa's ear, "this was our last chance. We can't get a hold of Molly and you have no identification—I mean there is no record of you anywhere on Earth, so how are we going to prove you're here?"

Suddenly, Moa smiles. "Because I'm not here."

"Remember you don't have powers of invisibility anymore!"

"Hillary," Moa whispers excitedly, "Maybe my power lies in the fact that I am undocumented! Follow my lead."

Hillary shakes her head in amazement, trying to imagine how Moa could possibly get them out of trouble.

Moa hops of her chair, strides confidently up to the officer and declares, "I want to see the king!"

The choice was upon me. However, as I stood outside the door, deep within the bowels of the stone temple, the fact that I could choose was far from my mind. Someone who needed help was in the confines of the room and with barely a thought, I opened the door.

Inside, a woman reclined on her side, feebly propping herself up on one hand. She was dressed in an ornate silk robe with a gold crown. She appeared to be both proud and downtrodden, as if years of toil and struggle had withered away at her vital well-being. It also appeared that she had been crying. So pitiful was her state that I rushed to her side only to discover that she was chained to the wall with thick metal cuffs, which were cutting into the thin flesh of her hands and feet.

"Please..." the word caught in her throat. "I...I'm so tired. You have vital life energy to heal. Can you please share it with me?"

Her glassy eyes darted from the door to me and then back again, as I examined the heavy cuff on her left wrist. It was iron and had dings, cuts, and scrapes all over. Perhaps this woman, in a stronger state, had tried in vain to break them off herself. I noticed her frail arms were weighed down and lifeless as I searched for the latch.

"Of course I will help you. I am a healer. My name is Ku," I said bravely. It filled my heart to be needed in this way.

"Yes, Ku. The villagers say you heal the sick. Your power is a glimmering gem within, the likes of which this world has never seen. I only need some of your healing power. I have worked so hard all my life and I am so tired, yet you are young and able."

"I have more than enough healing gifts to share," I said proudly and reached my hand out to examine one of her cuffs. It was hinged on one side and had a large keyhole on the other. Much to my surprise, it fell to the floor with a clunk.

Surprised at the ease with which my hapless, unnamed victim was freed, I touched the remaining three cuffs, which all fell to the floor in the same manner. When the final cuff was off, the woman leapt toward me and plunged her bony hand, her flowing red-silk sleeve fluttering behind, into my chest and extracted something—I wasn't quite sure what. The removal brought about a pain within me that was so deep, it traveled beyond my flesh and far into ancient portions of my soul. I felt helpless, powerless against this invasion. Within a blink of an eye, she held a glowing aquamarine jewel in her veined hand, which I instantly understood was the embodiment of all my healing abilities.

Then her body began to stretch, her face became a gnarled, knotted, unrecognizable mess. I watched as the frail woman morphed into a distended, flabby, slimy mass. Putrid brown ooze poured from what I could only guess was its eyes and mouth. A stench emanated from five large boils, which spurted frothy, yellow pus. The feeling that I got when this monster unveiled itself was almost worse that the disgusting visuals. I was overcome with despair, terror, and unfathomable loss. The combination of assault on my senses froze me on the spot.

"Help me!" I screamed.

Opening my mouth to scream again, my second attempt to call for help was stifled by one of three tentacles protruding from the monster's chest. The first wrapped around neck, then my mouth, the second curled around my arms, and the third cracked through my sternum with a force that brought tears to my eyes. When the tentacle emerged from my chest, it held my childhood essence. Within a flash of light, the essence was imprisoned in the glittering aquamarine jewel.

"You don't deserve the healing power contained within this jewel. I am much better suited to understand its true worth and to use it properly." The monster quickly dissolved into a bubbling blob, then disintegrated into nothing before my bewildered eyes.

I sat alone, empty, confused, and stunned. She had stolen the one thing I most valued and treasured, the thing that most defined who I was.

My heart pounded with panic as I ran from room to room, searching for the monster, trying, in desperation to retrieve that which was ripped from me—for without it, I was joyless, a shell of a person, not worthy of being on Earth.

The journey out of the temple brought to light a few pieces of information that I'd missed in my haste to be a savior. First, she hadn't called for me by name. I had assumed the responsibility for healing her was mine. I had delivered myself up to my own spiritual dismemberment. Second, the space in my soul, which had once contained my precious, coveted healing gifts, was now a gaping chasm. The open space caused an echoing, rattling, chaotic noise within my body and mind. The din was so loud that I could barely find my way through the circuitous frigid halls and back up the stone stairs.

*Why did the monster take something so essential to my existence on this Earth?* The question kept reverberating through my addled brain until I finally exited the temple. *And what was to become of me without it?*

With a convulsive jolt, I came back to consciousness from my meditation. I took a look around and was relieved to find that I was still on my special rock, and the sun was almost fully in the sky. *Perhaps*, I thought, *it was all just a journey of the mind, and all my gifts remained intact.*

I returned to my family's earthen-walled home and lay on my woven pallet. Through the front entry, framed with sturdy *kapok* limbs, I watched as my mother ground the *goji* berries and *pela* seeds into a nourishing paste. My one-month-old baby sister was nestled in her arms. Oh, how I wished to be in her place, protected by the warmth of my mother's arms. But not even these thoughts removed the rattling emptiness that now resided within my shattered soul. I drifted into a weary, troubled sleep.

As I slept, I dreamed that a baby monkey picked me like a flower and began pulling my petals off one by one, leaving my center exposed. The monkey whispered, "You are nothing without your soul, Ku. Let them take your body and save your family from peril."

My baby sister's piercing wail brought me to my senses and I awoke, leaping to my feet as a group of burly men tore their way through the thick brush surrounding our family's hut. Animals screeched, people ran in every direction and my family was nowhere to be seen, but from somewhere I could hear my baby sister's cry. My feet pounded the earth as I tried to put as much distance as possible between the terrifying scene and myself. I'd been told that marauders sometimes preyed on villages at night in search of food and water. Up until now, ours had been spared such invasions. I ran past my meditation spot, the clearing where I'd play hunter with my brothers—making as little noise as possible—and finally slowed as I saw a fallen majestic *kapok* tree. Normally, *kapoks* can live for up to one hundred years, and they provide a wide canopy of shade. However, this tree's massive but shallow root structure was exposed, and beneath it was a pocket large enough for me to squeeze my weary body and remain concealed. This is where I stayed until I saw the pink and orange glow of the rising sun.

Praying that whoever had attacked my village was long gone, I crept back to my village, the predawn light creating shadows on the tree limbs and waving leaves. Upon hearing the crunch of footsteps, I launched into a search for a secure hiding place. I tried to push out any thoughts of what might have happened to my family—when I remembered the cave my father had shown me. It was virtually hidden from view and contained several dark roomy pockets, which were only accessible through a small crawl space. This, I was sure, was where my brothers, baby sister, mother, and father were. When I played, I often pretended I was a tiger, and this is how I entered the cave on the outskirts of my eerily silent village.

# CHAPTER IV

# Breath of Fire

### Ritual: Slaying the Dragon
### Stone: Yellow Citrine
### Blend: Gem Elixir

---

*Sit or stand in a crowd. Your choice of venue can be outside in nature or inside at an event, shopping area, or restaurant. Wherever you are, make sure you have time to quiet your mind with three breaths. Allow your body to relax with each inhale and imagine that any fear, worry, negativity or stress exits your body as you exhale. Then imagine an energy emanating from within your body, which extends about two feet around you. This energy is your aura and you can control all that is within your unique energetic boundary. Examine your aura. What does it feel like? Any colors? Does it have any specific scent, taste, sound? Bring your awareness to those around you. Close your eyes. Every person around you has an aura. It grows and shrinks around the body to accommodate or defend the physical body. See your own aura pulsating with life, energy, and protection. Now imagine that someone in the crowd approaches you and stands five feet away. Then they are two feet away. Now imagine them right in front of you. A light emanates from your heart, shoots out to the edge of your aura, and creates a light barrier. The person's aura hits the outside of your light barrier and slips off. It is your choice to allow other people's energies to commingle with your own.*

*Blessed Be.*

Moa stands before the officer, her hands on her small hips.

"The king?" The crisply uniformed officer opens his mouth, pulls his lips back, and spews a vicious stream of laughter. Then he snaps sharply, "Sit." He points to the row of chairs. "You speak again, you dead."

The girls dare not make another request. The image of being yanked from their seats, thrown into a Jeep, driven to a nondescript location, and shot dead is enough to squelch any more "plans."

"Oh, God," Hillary whispers to Moa, "we're dead."

Despite the upsetting situation, Moa seems calm. "I can't explain what will happen, I just know everything will be okay."

"How? The butterfly?" Hillary's voice sounds pinched, "Moa, you don't have your old powers, you can't disappear or make yourself invisible...you can't sign official documents or make..."

"Hillary, maybe the officer didn't hear my request, but perhaps someone else—the people who will grant it—did hear me. Sometimes the simple act of speaking up can be enough to change the course of events."

The two settle into an anxious silence.

Hour upon hour passes. The sun disappears and an even more frightening officer replaces the prim one. This new deputy doesn't even look at the girls. The stench of stale cigarettes wafts from his clothing, and every few minutes he lets out a mucous-filled cough. Eventually Hillary and Moa fall asleep. Moa's head nestles into the curve of Hillary's neck, and Hillary's cheek rests atop Moa's soft hair.

A bang from the door startles the two from their slumber. The new officer doesn't even look up. Before they are fully awake, the two are handcuffed and forced out the door into the burning sunlight. It's the next day!

Their escort is an enormous and frightening man with thick forearms and thicker biceps. Covered from head to toe in monochromatic tan fatigues, he directs the two shocked girls with gruff movements. In silence, he guides them with an occasional poke in the back with his monstrous machine gun. A lump rises in Hillary's throat and she summons the courage from far beyond this moment when, she hopes and prays, she and Moa will be safe. For now, she swallows hard and pushes the pulsating lump of fear back down into her tight chest.

Still shackled, they squeeze into the backseat of an army Jeep. The machine gun is set upright in the passenger's seat—a frightening reminder of who truly has all the power in this mysterious adventure gone awry. Hillary slips her hand into Moa's and gives it a squeeze. She guesses it is late morning by the direction of the sun. The hot wind whips her hair around her eyes and nose and despite her fear, she is grateful for the change of scenery. Moa is unusually quiet. She presses palm to chest in an effort to quell the fluttering thump of her heart and her eyes focus on an invisible reference point beyond her current reality.

After a ten-minute drive on an empty desert road, Moa gasps, "Hillary, is that what I think it is?"

In front of them is a limestone tunnel, which descends directly into the earth. Beyond the tunnel's entrance, the sandy dirt looks untouched, as if nothing unusual might exist below.

Hillary scans the horizon for any indication of where the tunnel might lead, but sees only sand dunes and rock piles. It feels to her as if no one has touched the desert for thousands of years.

The driver flips on the headlights which barely illuminate the road ahead, and the Jeep and its passengers are plunged into near darkness. The only sound is the chugging engine and the only light comes from the yellowish gray headlamps. Moa inhales the tang of fear mixed with ancient musty clay and chokes back a sob.

Hillary pushes back her own rising panic and squeezes Moa's little fingers tighter, looping her right arm around Moa's neck and pulling her close. Then she extends her left arm in front of Moa, creating a human shield for the little girl. If something should hit them from the front, it will hit Hillary first.

The girls travel in almost complete darkness, the gravel clanking on the Jeep's undercarriage. Then the car's tires thump onto a much smoother surface and a circle of sunlight appears in the distance, which gradually grows larger until they reemerge at the far edge of a glorious royal compound.

Hillary and Moa blink as their eyes readjust to the noonday sun. A compound with thirteen buildings of varying sizes and shapes bubbles up from the sand. The structure's roofs are shiny jewels on the horizon. The largest structure is a palace with a gleaming gold dome on top. The surrounding buildings are scattered around the main palace. Hillary exhales as she takes in the glittering structural landscape of lapis lazuli, ruby, and diamonds.

"The palace! They are buildings, but they look like..." Moa shouts.

"Gemstones!" Hillary unwinds her arm from around Moa and lets her clap her hands with glee.

It takes another twenty minutes to reach the palace, and the palace compound becomes more awe inspiring with each passing mile. All the while, Hillary tries to wrap her mind around the reality of Moa's request actually being granted.

Moa bounces up and down in her seat, "I get to meet the King of Egypt!" Then sings at the top of her lungs, "We are going...la, la, la...to see the king...la, la, la..."

The driver moves his thick hairy hand toward the passenger's seat in the direction of the machine gun, which immediately stops Moa from her joyous refrain. Then he reaches his hand deep into the crevice where the back of the Jeep's leather seat meets the well-worn seat and removes something, tossing the extracted item into the backseat. Hillary spies a flash of color as the item bounces off of her lap and onto the dusty floor.

Moa and Hillary are agape. Below their feet is a pair of sunglasses that are identical to the ones given to Hillary at the store in Honolulu by a cantankerous store clerk. They are made of thick plastic and, although sturdy, they are a mishmash of neon colors. These glasses make it possible to see the Anuenue. Since neither Hillary nor Moa can reach the sunglasses, they can only speculate about what this unexpected sign means.

The Jeep pulls through an ornate marble arch with a built-in guard shack at its base. The uniformed guard types on a computer as the driver steers onto a heavy marble–block driveway. Carved marble statues line the driveway on the way up to the palace's front entrance. Each hand-hewn statue has its own expression and duty. Moa takes in the grandeur as they pass granite servants, guards, and officers, all of whom seem at the ready to serve, protect, defend whoever is worthy enough to tread upon royal soil. Hillary sits up a little straighter, imagining the dignitaries, kings, and queens who have driven through this same palace entrance.

The entrance to the palace is breathtaking. Lush vines line a shady stone walkway, which is draped with soft, opaque, cream-colored linen cloth. The guard helps the girls out of the Jeep, takes out a key, and unlocks their handcuffs. Hillary is the first to be unshackled and as Moa is freed, she reaches into the backseat and grabs the sunglasses from the floor.

The driver points to the walkway, "I cannot escort you past this point. You must go alone." With that, he hops back into the Jeep and speeds off, a cloud of dust billowing behind.

"I wonder why the Anuenue want us set free?" Hillary says as she places the sunglasses on her face and looks toward the departing vehicle.

"Why?" Moa gives a cough as dust blows around their heads.

"Because our driver is one of them." Hillary hands the glasses to Moa. She can just make out the bright colors of the telltale Anuenue shirt as the Jeep disappears into the shimmering desert.

The walkway feels smooth on Moa's feet and she slips her hand into Hillary's. Smiling at each other, they glide along to the luxuriously designed entrance. Before them is the residence of King Emel Shanheer, a blood descendant of King Tutankhamen and the royal family.

"Well, Moa." Hillary inhales the dry leafy scent. "Let's hope King Shanheer is understanding about our difficult position."

Moa is caught up in the grandeur of the moment and of the regal surroundings. It is overwhelming to imagine that her wish had been granted and to acknowledge that she is finally on a path—literally and figuratively—to regaining ownership of her mother's statue.

Marble, stone, and inlaid ornate tile work cover every section of the palace facade. Moa tries to imagine how such detailed artistry was accomplished and how long it might have taken. The closer they get to the entrance the more Moa notices the painstakingly precise workmanship. There are patches of grass on either side of the walkway, and each blade looks like it has been measured and hand cut.

Topiaries flank the front door and they pause, looking for a way to announce their arrival. This front door is the granddaddy of doors, with an immense wooden frame and curved metal piping outlining opaque yellow glass, which glows brightly. Hillary tries to imagine what could possibly be behind such a marvelous door. Moa searches for a handle or a doorbell, but there is none. Just then, the door slowly swings in and Hillary and Moa stand gaping.

"OH!" Hillary screams.

It's not the sunlit atrium or the polished hand-carved mahogany banister that has caused her to cry out, but the sight of Molly and Heidi dressed from head to toe in ornate Egyptian sarongs and draped with jewels.

As I sat in the dark, I tried to imagine where my family could be. I'd searched every inch of the dark pocket, which was located deep within the cave, but no one was there. My mind began to play tricks on me. Three times I thought I heard twigs snap, and I held my breath and waited for the inevitable capture from my village's marauders, but it never came. Even if my family didn't make it to this cave, I prayed that they had escaped harm. Finally, desperation to know of my family's whereabouts took over and I gathered up my courage, slowly scooted out of the crawl space backward, and made my way back to the village.

Blinking in the sunlight, I took in the material damage. My family's home had been split open like a nut, its outer shell broken in large pieces. My family—thankfully—was nowhere near it. I explored the village's common areas and saw that some families were not so lucky. A bolt of terror ran through me like an electric shock as I discovered a playmate of mine and his younger brother lying next to each other, their heads in the same state as my family home, blood surrounding each body like a moat. My hands shook as I performed my healing ritual. Neither responded and I sadly realized that they had been gone too long.

Heaviness overtook my heart as I tried to remove from my mind's eye the awful sight I'd just witnessed. I swallowed the feeling of rising bile in my throat. But then I encountered the bodies of a young mother and her toddler clinging to one another, a death mask of horror frozen on each of their faces. I experienced a feeling of desperation, as if those who had caused this living nightmare had left behind a purple mist which permeated my being, my very soul, extinguishing all hope and, I was certain, my inner light. Much to my own shame, instead of attempting to heal the mother and child, I ran to the far end of the village and stopped at a glen just at its entrance.

The forest was quiet, for all animals had gone far from the bloodbath. Out of the corner of my eye, I saw a movement in the brush and immediately hid, praying for protection, just as I had in the cave.

The gurgle made me jump. It was right behind me and I turned to discover my older brother, barely alive, blood streaming from a gash on is right temple. I pulled his head into my lap and performed my healing ritual. As I prayed for healing light, he said, "Mama, Pap, Juju, and Sissy are gone. I love you, Ku." And then he was gone. This was okay, I thought, I have been able to bring some back from death. The reason I couldn't bring back my playmate and his brother was because they had been dead for far too long and their souls had left their bodies. I created a healing chamber of amber and crystals, invoking light. But my brother did not move.

No, I thought, I cannot lose them all. "Heal!" I screamed. "I can heal you."

I continued on for who knows how long…hours, minutes…still my brother's hand turned cold. I anointed him with my tears—touching his forehead, his throat, his chest.

But my healing gifts were really gone as was my brother and I was alone.

# CHAPTER V

# True Desires

## Ritual: Core Healing
## Stone: Ruby
## Blend: Resonance Elixir

---

*Sit cross-legged on a patch of earth. It can be anywhere as long as your body is in contact with the ground. Take three gentle breaths to calm your mind. After your last exhale, take an inhaling hum. Exhale normally and take another inhaling hum breath. (It will sound like an audible gasp.) As you do so, imagine that the vibration you are creating starts in your nasal cavity and travels all around your head.*
*Your inhaling hum is your personal vibration of hope.*

*Allow hope to permeate every cell of your being.*
*Choose hope as your divine guide.*

*Blessed Be.*

Moa runs, arms open wide toward Molly and Heidi, and when she reaches them wraps one arm around Molly's waist and the other around Heidi's shoulders.

"Are you really here?" Hillary arrives seconds after Moa and puts one arm around Molly and another on Heidi's head, stroking her hair.

"We've been waiting for you." Heidi says gleefully.

She and Moa hold hands and take turns squeezing each other so hard they lift each other off the ground. Then they run in circles screaming,

"Aaaaaaaaaaahhhhhhhhh!" they shout at the top of their lungs. The noise reverberates off of the vaulted ceiling and resounds through the hallways.

"You look gorgeous, Mol." Hillary tries to speak over the din and gives her sister a squeeze. "What are you doing here?"

"You're never going to believe it. A car showed up in front of our house…"

Because of the noise, the two women don't notice that a young man in his early twenties has been approaching until he is right upon them. Hillary starts, then regains her composure. He is the most serene man she has ever seen, with smooth, beautiful skin and thickly lashed dark eyes that flash the unusual colors of green, purple, and blue.

"I wanted to give you all a family moment. Hello, I am Syret Meh. Call me M." He extends his hand to Hillary. The customary handshake, however, goes on about three seconds too long.

The girls, now done with their celebrating, join the group by holding hands and running full force at Hillary and Molly. Heidi yells, "Running hug!" The impact knocks the women back as the girls dissolve into giggles.

"I'm Hillary." She smiles and then looks down, studying the pattern on the oriental runner beneath her feet. Warmth rises in her cheeks as they turn bright pink.

M leads the group toward a sunken sitting area with a brocade-tufted sofa, two armchairs, and several ottomans. Three sets of French doors are opened to reveal a tiered patio area overlooking a reflecting pool and a series of fountains. Two marble obelisks flank a wooden bust of the Egyptian god Thoth—god of knowledge and writing—and palms, ferns, and ornamental grasses shade other ancient statues of gods and goddesses. In the center is a lone golden silk meditation pillow, which sits atop a wooden riser. Outside, a hammock big enough for four people swings lightly in the midafternoon breeze. The whole garden welcomes anyone who visits this special place with a sense of spirituality, otherworldliness, peace, and comfort.

"Please make yourselves comfortable." M motions to the sunken sitting area.

Molly slides in next to her sister on a small sofa with yellow silk hummingbirds. M sits next to the woman on the matching *peau de soie* ottoman. The girls squeeze into a suede armchair. Then he directs his gaze toward Hillary. "My father, King Emel Shanheer, left this morning for Shanghai, but he authorized diplomatic status for you and Moa before his departure."

"Why would he do that?" Hillary says warily.

"Who cares?" Moa jumps up off of the chair. "Where's the Statue of Ku?"

"Moa," Hillary rises and takes Moa's arm. "I know you want to find your mother's statue, but I need to know why they are allowing an undocumented girl into their country." As attractive as this man is, she still feels guarded. So she directs her next question right into his sparkling eyes. "Why did you fly my sister and niece here?"

M rises to meet her gaze. "Hillary, I know you and Moa have been through a lot over the last twenty-four hours…"

An uncomfortable silence is broken by the sound of echoing footsteps. It's the Guardian, who is now dressed in a more ornate uniform. He looks very regal in this ivory suit, which has gold braiding along the outside of each pant leg and features colorful medals and ribbons on the jacket's left lapel.

"Excuse me, M. I am at your disposal to escort Miss Hillary and Miss Moa to their wing if you'd like." His demeanor is even more formal that before, and M gives an equally formal nod.

The Guardian's heels click on the floor as Molly, Heidi, Hillary, and Moa follow him through a gargantuan archway, which leads to a fifty-foot atrium.

"Whoa!" Moa yells, her voice echoing for a full minute.

"Isn't it cool?" Heidi chimes in. "Echo! She and Moa begin an echo game each trying to out echo the other.

"ECHO!"

"ECHO!"

"GIRLS, PLEASE!" Molly's voice immediately stops the girls.

The domed ceiling has swirls of stars and planets. Walls on either side are lined with windows overlooking a manicured lawn.

Hillary shields her eyes from the blinding, laser-like shard of light emanating from the peak of the cupola, then whispers to Molly, "Can you imagine growing up in a place like this?"

The Guardian smiles. "Your rooms will be in the Bahariya Oasis Wing." He escorts them through French doors leading to an inviting and intimate seating area with six doors.

Hillary and Moa are given separate rooms next to each other. Heidi and Molly are staying across the seating area in their own rooms, which overlook a lap pool and tennis court. Hillary's and Moa's rooms each have a stone balcony overlooking a lush Japanese garden. Hillary takes in the serenity of the elements in the garden. A wooden bridge arches above a thin, winding creek. On a small berm above the creek sits a stone fountain flanked by six beautiful bonsai trees. Nestled between the water, the stone fountain, and the wood bridge is an ancient iron Shinto shrine. Hillary tries to imagine the meticulous care that has gone into maintaining this breathtaking garden.

Turning her attention back to her room, Hillary runs her hand over a beautiful white-painted dresser.

Heidi has been following Moa around with a running commentary. "We got to swim in the pool. And look!" Heidi opens Moa's closet to reveal a closet full of gorgeous clothes. "They are all your size and completely beeeeeaaauuutiful!"

"Incredible!" Moa laughs.

Heidi is on to the next subject. "What do you see outside? Ooooh, look at that waterfall!"

"Isn't it divine!" Moa follows Heidi as she opens a door to gleefully discover that it leads to Hillary's room.

"Hi!" The girls skip over to Hillary, who is on her own balcony talking with Molly. For a brief moment they take in the peaceful garden sights and sounds.

"I don't get it," Hillary breaks the silence. "Why would they fly you and Heidi here, Mol? Why give us all this? Something is not right."

"You sound like me, Hil." Molly laughs and gives her sister a nudge. "They have been completely hospitable. And M told me that he really needs our help. That's why we're here."

"While we're here, we might as well have a little fun!" Moa says, then turns and does a running leap onto Hillary's bed. The frame is hand painted and matches the dresser, and its headboard and footboard are both embroidered with textured verdant, green silk. Heidi follows Moa into the bed with a cannonball jump.

"Wheeee!" Heidi yells as a ray of sunlight hits the gold trim of the cobalt-blue duvet and shoots sparkles throughout the room.

A new distraction catches Moa's eye. "Books!" She bounds off the bed and practically hugs a glass-fronted bookcase.

"I love books, too!" Heidi taps on the glass, then gives the cabinet doors a gentle tug. "Shoot, it's locked. Those books look so old and there's one on ancient Egypt. Oh, now I really want to read that crumbly old book."

Molly gives Hillary a smile. Anytime her child is excited about reading is fine with her.

A knock at the door interrupts the play. Heidi and Moa scramble off the bed and race to see who can get there first. Moa wins and opens the door with a flourish. "Come in!"

"I bring you an invitation for dinner with the prince." A young man dressed in a brocade top and pants hands Moa the thick, embossed stationery and bows on his way out.

"Excuse me," Heidi says loudly, but the heavy door is already closing as the young man pads down the hallway.

"We get to dress up and go to a fancy dinner!" Moa jumps up and down, "This is a dream come true!"

Heidi joins her. "I'll ask the prince about a key to the bookcase. Come on Moa. Let's get dressed." They run back into Moa's room to pick out a gorgeous dinner ensemble.

"Good," Hillary says, grateful that the girls will have a project to distract them while she does some real detective work. With that, she opens the closet and stifles a gasp. It is filled with an entire wardrobe of women's clothing, sorted by color. Casual shirts hang on the left-top section and casual pants and skirts hang below. Grabbing an aqua blouse with ruffles and a sequined gray skirt, she holds them up. They are both her size. Hillary runs her hand along the luscious dress fabrics. Her fingers slip through a filmy beige-pink chiffon cocktail dress lined with soft, light-blue silk, a shimmery gold, satin minidress, and a gorgeous black-lace ball gown. With a flourish, she pulls out a silk cocktail dress with cap sleeves, jeweled neckline, and bell skirt and holds it up for Molly to see.

With a nod of approval Molly says, "I have a similarly gorgeous array of clothing in my closet, too." Then, almost as an afterthought she says, "M really has been a wonderful host, Hil."

Hillary steels herself. "I'm still interested in knowing why he has allowed a little girl with no identification into his country." And then, Hillary remembers why she and Moa are here. "Oh, and where the Statue of Ku is as well." But as Hillary turns away, she feels her cheeks growing hot again, thinking of the prince and his startling eyes.

The memory of my brother's bloody, gurgling pleas for help replayed in my mind as I grabbed my father's hunting sack and prepared to fill it with provisions. To dissolve the horrific pictures burned into my brain, I summon a memory from my early childhood. The first one I can remember is of my father preparing for a hunting trip. Before a hunt, he would make an offering of a wild hare to Neith, the goddess of war and hunting. Then he would anoint the bag, himself, and whoever was chosen to travel out that day.

It was an honor to be selected to travel out into the night and gather food for our family. The choice seemed arbitrary, but my father always seemed to pick the person who was most in need of time alone with him. I was still too young to actually go on the hunt, but my father would allow me to help him pack for his journey. He'd check and recheck all the provisions to ensure that he and his aide would have enough food to survive for the weeklong trip.

In spite of my attempts to forget, the excruciating picture reemerged, in my mind's eye, of my brother gasping for his last breath. A wash of shame overtook me as I, once again, pushed the thought away with my father's words. "Strength, balance," he would say, as he brushed his thick hair out of his eyes and carefully checked my packing, "and economy make a good hunter."

I rolled up a woven reed mat, silently wishing my father was here to check my work, then shoved a gazelle pelt, which my mother had pounded soft, into the bottom of the sack. These items would be the only memories of home. There were enough berries, dried meat, and cheese to last me a week. By then, hopefully I'd find a new place to live or, at least, more food. Last, I found a pliant, oiled, animal hide made into a pouch. My mother used to transport water for her food preparation with this watertight device. I plotted my course and decided that my first stop would be our family's usual watering spot, a lovely brook that was a half-day's walk. At least I thought it was that far. My mother told stories after her return and described the lush foliage that lined the brook. I never went with her, but thought it might be fitting to do her homage by putting a remembrance of her at the water's edge.

The birds gave me a loud send-off as I strode out of the village, the only home I'd known, and out into the wilderness. My father had told me stories of his childhood in the jungle, tales of his heroic conquests of zebras, gazelles, and the occasional rhinoceros. His expression would darken as he described the dwindling water supply and his continuing effort to divine more water.

Outside our village, the terrain was transforming. Rivers were drying up, towns were migrating, and people were becoming extremely desperate. I reached our family's usual watering spot and found a trickle. I imagined what my father's reaction would be at my discovery and shuddered at the thought of his ominous, furrowed brow. Oh, how I missed him! So I followed the trickle to a small puddle-sized pond with enough water to fill my pouch. If I followed the creek bed, I reasoned, I would be able to survive with whatever water I found, which might last me on my journey. Surely by then I'd find other encampments.

Soon I had traveled well beyond any recognizable rocks or trees. I followed a dry creek bed; its smooth rocks and cracked dirt surface were a change from the dry grass and rocky shards in the brush.

On the first night, I snuggled under the warm gazelle pelt and cried myself to sleep. By morning I had awakened with a renewed energy and continued my trek. I followed creek beds, animal tracks, and droppings, all in hope of finding water and people.

At last I sucked the final drops of water from my pouch and plodded on toward a tall grove of trees in the distance. When I arrived, I cleared out an area under a large bush, just large enough for me to fit. The top created a canopy and I felt protected within the leaves and twigs. There were no more tears that evening as I drifted off.

Days passed and I was able to find a few sips of water from within plant bulbs and gourds. The land became rockier and drier than I had ever seen.

I climbed a tall rock and looked out at the stretch of land before me. There were miles and miles of sand. It was as if I'd come to the end of the world.

At the edge of this desert, I saw a man with a long beard, and a cloth wrapped around his head to keep the sun away. He had a walking stick and moved slowly, steadily. I decided to sit on top of the rock and watch him, for it had been days since I'd seen a living soul and I was so lonely for comfort.

The closer he got, the lonelier I became. Since my healing and sensory powers were gone, I had no ability to connect with my guides and angels. It was as if they had vanished completely. Anxious to connect with another human, I gathered my bag, climbed down the rock, and walked toward him.

His eyes caught hold of my presence when I was only a few yards away. His expression never changed, but I decided to smile anyway. He was almost certainly taller than me but had a severely hunched back, which brought him down almost to my height.

"Hello!" I said.

He made a grunting sound and walked right up to me, bringing his face inches away from mine. It was as if he was examining every pore of my face.

"I am Ku. Son of Shimar, from the village of Tet."

Then, with a perfunctory nod, he said, "Come with me."

I followed him toward a rust-colored string of hills. We walked until the sun was barely visible, a sliver of orange light peeking between two reddish mounts.

The old man pointed a crooked finger at a shelter outside of the main building and said, "You sleep there." Then he went inside.

Grateful for the hope of company, I followed his orders. The room was quite large and the floor was covered in dried grass. I gathered some up into the corner and put my woven mat down. The night was getting chilly, so I pulled on my pelt for cover as I'd done for many nights before. *I'd finally made it to safety!*

The next morning, I awoke to the man standing above me and poking me with his walking stick. "Food is over there."

He pointed to a flat stone with some freshly cooked meat on it. Not knowing or caring of its origin, I gobbled it up quickly, even licking the stone until it was clean.

A fresh pail of water had been put just inside the door and I drank from a hollowed out gourd floating on top. What luck to be in such lavish surroundings. Surely my life would turn around even if I no longer had my healing abilities.

Once I had eaten and drunk my fill, I stepped outside to explore. There I found the man and an older boy who was pointing and talking about a stretch of earth.

"I am Fet," said the old man. "This is Hap." He pointed to the gangly boy who appeared a few years older than I. Neither smiled at the introduction.

The two continued talking about the earth, seeds, and growth patterns, while I wandered around the field kicking at stones. The ground looked scorched and dusty, as if the sun had sucked layer upon layer of water and left only minerals, clay, and sand. Then I noticed a young girl on the outer edge of the field. She sifted and pulled, throwing out the occasional rock.

Fet called me over. "You clear land. Girl will show you how." He pointed to the girl in the field.

The girl's name was Am. She was seven years old, too, and her parents had sold her to Fet when she was four. She was meant to be his concubine, but since she was too young, Fet made her work for her board and meals in the field.

It seemed like a fair arrangement, me helping him for food and shelter. Am's arrangement made me shudder.

The tiny farm was far from any other people and on the edge of a vast desert. The only company I had was Fet, Hap, and Am. Fet was not much of a conversationalist, but Hap was an entirely different story. He was chatty to the point of being annoying and was a know-it-all, to boot. Hap was in charge of caring for Fet's animals—five goats, four sheep, and two pigs—and his hut was on the opposite end of the property.

One day, I received a lesson about Hap's nature. I saw that the goat needed water and so I walked to the creek to get water for the animals. When I returned, Hap was angry, but instead of yelling at me, he turned to Fet and told him that I wasn't worth having around anymore.

I didn't hear Hap speak with Fet in front of me, but overheard them as I came from the fields to get a few sips of water.

Fet's grumpy demeanor turned even sourer as days turned into weeks, but strangely instead of letting me go free, he kept me on.

I don't look back on those days in terms of happiness and sadness, but more as an emergence out of suffering. After a period of grief, the work and the shelter it provided, was sliver of hope. At the time, I was simply appreciative of the company. My days were spent clearing the sandy soil of rocks and weeds, and my evenings were spent in the loving peaceful company of the animals.

Fet would sit in front of his house and drink a fermented broth out of a thick metal cup. He'd bark orders to Hap and had pretty much stopped speaking to me, which was fine with me. His voice would send an electric shock of fear through me every time he called, so honestly I was relieved to have a break from dealing with him.

Hap would occasionally join me in the fields, but for the most part he became the boss, telling me where to clear and what I was doing wrong. Am was the bright spot in my days. After work, we would return from the field, all tired and dusty, and take turns telling stories. She was an amazing story weaver. Her colorful tales of the desert kept me riveted for hours. I would share my stories of the jungle and the animals we encountered. Together, we helped each other sustain some version of normalcy.

Fet never yelled at me, he never beat me, but I could tell that his hatred grew with every day I worked on his farm. It was just a sense, a dark feeling within my depths that sent a jolt through me whenever I saw him. If Fet wanted to communicate a message to me, he would speak through Hap. Trouble was, I never knew if Hap was making up his own rules or regurgitating Fet's.

One day, there was no mistaking that Fet had set a rule that I had unwittingly broken. For almost a year I'd worked in the fields, and on this day he sang a song to pass the time. Suddenly, Hap was pulling me by the ear to Fet's perch.

Upon my arrival, Fet stared at me with only a slight hint of distain, as Hap snidely whispered, "No singing."

Fet's reaction brought up more fear within me than Hap's. Beneath Fet's look of stolid distain lurked immeasurable fury. If he hated me, then why didn't he let me go free? Surely, sending me to fend for myself out in the endless desert would satisfy him.

I began to get headaches at night and found that sitting, as I used to do, on a large boulder in the moonlight and concentrating on my breath gave me comfort. Even though the meditations no longer brought me guidance, I decided to continue them because they provided me with a sense of peace and healing. Thus I began the first step to healing my soul. Am asked to join me one evening and together we sat quietly.

One evening I snuck into Fet's home hoping to learn more about him. The more I understood about my captor, I reasoned, the more power I had. Am knew very little about her master, and Hap, if he knew, certainly wasn't going to tell. Quietly I looked around Fet's room. The home was divided into three areas, with earthen walls dividing a living area, sleeping area, and eating area. As I entered into the home, I peered in at him on his soft grass mat as he slept. The sight was grotesque. His mouth was open and drool spilled out of the corner of one mouth. But I found nothing to reveal why he hated me. Dozens of metal cups—very rare and expensive in our area—caught my attention. These were hand molded and stamped with his seal, a large X with a snake slithering up one side. It must have taken him years to collect this many.

The work in the fields was tiring, but even more difficult was that Fet and Hap seemed to enjoy ignoring me. Am could spend some time with me, but Fet saw to it that our contact was limited.

Early on in my stay and long after Am had returned to her pallet on the far side of the land, I would lie outside and look up at the stars and weep for all I had lost. It was late into one of my crying sessions that I heard a tiny sound that stopped my crying. Following the tiny noise, I crept through the brush and saw a small, shivering animal tucked into a tight crouch. In the moonlight, I could just make out the outline of a baby monkey's back and long thin arms as well as its tail. The tiny animal whimpered and sniffed. Out of instinct, I reached out to pet the poor thing and sooth its obvious fear. As my hand touched its head, the monkey nipped at me.

My reflexes were quick and he only got the air. But I sat back and looked at this wee creature. Upon closer examination, I saw that its ribs were showing and that it was extremely malnourished, so I crept back to my hut and found a few morsels of grain and brought a gourd of water with me back to the cowering animal. When I held out the bits, the poor thing grabbed them and snatched the gourd so hastily that water splashed onto the ground. The little one guzzled and gulped the water until it was gone, then it scurried into a hole at the base of a tree without so much as a glance in my direction.

You're welcome, I thought. And headed back onto my pad to sleep.

CHAPTER VI

# The Book

## Ritual: Blessing the Emotions
## Stone: Aquamarine
## Elixir Spray: Geranium Essence Elixir

*Find a safe place to lie flat on your back and close your eyes where you will be uninterrupted. Imagine you are lying on a soft beach with an ocean at your feet. The water has special powers. As the tide ebbs and flows, imagine that it reaches your feet and ebbs, it flows to your knees and ebbs, and then it reaches your shoulders and ebbs. When these special waters make contact with your body, you will forever be transformed. The water will pull out stuck emotions that you have held onto, either accidentally or on purpose.*

*The reason that emotions get stuck in our body is because we believe we can own them.*

*Feelings are not meant to be possessed. Each day you experience a variety of emotions and those, which you choose to hold, may block other feelings from coming in.*
*No matter the reason, see any obstructions in the flow of your emotions washing away into the vast magical sea.*

*(At no time do these waters cover your face.) As the waves ebb and flow, making their way up to your head, allow any unexpressed emotions out. Scream into a pillow, hit it with your fists, cry, laugh. Expression is transformation.*

*You are not your emotions.*

*Blessed Be.*

Before Heidi, Moa, Molly, and Hillary enter the sparkling dining room, they pass by the seating area with the gorgeous garden area. Moa's hair has been put up into a French twist and she wears a royal-blue, silk sheath dress, which is tied at the waist with matching braided belt. She is so enthralled with the entrancing garden, she nearly runs into Hillary, who is now showered and dressed in her lovely midnight-blue cocktail dress.

"I want to come back out here and play after dinner," Moa declares as she gazes longingly at the tinkling fountains and the lush greenery. "I want to swing in the hammock."

"Sounds good to me." Hillary takes Heidi's and Moa's hands as they follow a woman dressed in a black pantsuit.

The woman directs Heidi and Molly to sit on the far side of the table and Hillary and Moa to sit across from them.

"The prince will be with you shortly." She looks over their heads as if she's speaking to a stadium full of fans.

The table is big enough to seat twenty people. Hillary speaks up, "It's a little strange, don't you think, that we are crammed onto one end of this huge table? Perhaps the hostess was addressing the other sixteen invisible people."

"Well, what would you like, Hillary?" Molly uses Hillary's full name when she is irked. "We could sit at the far end of the table and yell to you. Would you prefer that?"

M enters and greets each one, then sits down at the head of the table.

"You'll have to excuse me." He slips into his chair as a lanky male server, dressed in a black tunic and pants, closes the door. "I was dealing with some business issues."

An uncomfortable silence follows. Finally Heidi blurts, "Can we get the key to the bookcase in Hillary's room? It has some really cool old books in it, but it's locked. Oh, and Hillary wants to know why you let Moa in with no ID."

Embarrassed at Heidi's outburst, but glad to have the issue of the missing identification out in the open, Hillary clears her throat and adds, "Yes. You never answered my question from early this afternoon."

"Oh, yes, the bookcase key." The prince's eyes dance and he exchanges nods with an older gentleman who exits to locate the missing key. "As for Moa, her…" he searches for the correct word, "…status makes her an ideal candidate for retrieving the Statue of Ku."

"What 'status' is that?" Hillary asks as she watches a female server ladle soup into the bowl.

"Just what I told you while we were being detained. I am not here!" Moa grabs the soup ladle and splashes soup in her own bowl. Much to everyone's surprise, she doesn't spill a drop.

The prince continues. "Moa, because of your undocumented status, you can gain access and move about our country without being traced. We have an idea of who has the statue, but we need your help to retrieve it."

Heidi and Molly watch the conversation play out like it is on television.

Hillary finally looks at Molly. "Did you know about this?"

"No." Molly sounds defensive and avoids Hillary's gaze.

"Aren't you the slightest bit curious about why you are here?" Hillary is angry now. "I am responsible for Moa and even if no one else cares, I will not let her be taken advantage of. She's just a little girl!" She rises to go, but the prince stands, too.

"Hillary. I understand your frustration. But if you and Moa would have tried searching for the statue by yourselves, how far do you think you would have gotten?"

The prince did have a point. Hillary stayed where she was.

He continues, "My family can offer you protection and comforts you would not otherwise be able to afford."

Hillary remains standing. "We could just go back to Hawaii, you know."

"No, we can't," Heidi breaks in, "We don't have any money."

Molly looks at the floor. Her cheeks are flushed and her eyes well up. In the uncomfortable silence, the truth suddenly dawns on Hillary.

"Mol, why didn't you tell me?" Hillary crosses to Molly's side, leans down, and gives her a hug.

"We are upside down with our mortgage." Molly begins to cry. "I'm so sorry, Hil. They told us that if we helped you find the statue, they'd pay off our house."

Hillary walks over to the prince. "I can't believe you would put a young mother and her daughter in this position. We will find the statue on our own and when we do, we'll have the satisfaction of knowing that we are kind, loving people who did not bow to imperialism." Hillary takes a step toward the door, but turns to express one last thought. "You have more money than any of us will ever have, and you could buy thousands of antiquities just like it. Why do you even care about this one little statue?"

Hillary walks back to her bedroom and waits to hear the click of Molly's heels and taps of Heidi and Moa feet. She is famished, so she snacks on a few items from a gift basket left on a sideboard at her room's entrance. She munches an apple and a handful of almonds, but is still hungry. After all, she hasn't eaten in a full day. She is about to go back to the dining room to get something to eat when there is a knock at the door.

She is surprised and relieved to see a male server holding a tray filled with food. Thanking him, she grabs the tray and heads out on the balcony to enjoy the cool evening breeze, as she devours the hearty lamb stew, roasted potatoes, and pureed squash. She is so distracted by the food that she doesn't notice the note with her name on the envelope, until she has almost eaten her fill.

*Hillary,*

*Please accept my apologies. You are correct to question my family's motives. This situation is new to you and you deserve time to get to know us and proceed at your own pace. You, your sister, friend, and niece may remain our guests for as long as you wish.*

*So far, the only clue we know of the statue's location is that it was mistakenly sent to an import company. We know it is somewhere in Egypt but have no idea where. My only request is that if or when you do find the Statue of Ku, you allow us to view it before you take it back to Hawaii.*

*Respectfully, M*

Hillary is astonished. This offer seems too good to be true. There must be a trap. She entertains the thought of leaving without the statue, but knows that Moa would never go for that. And she would never leave Moa. Then she thinks of Molly and Heidi. She had no idea their financial situation was so dire. She would hate to have her stubbornness cause Molly and Heidi to lose their house.

As she slips between the luxurious Egyptian cotton sheets, she finalizes her decision. For the present, she'll stay and explore. After all, she managed to save the island of Hawaii with Molly's, Heidi's, and Moa's help. Surely they ought to be able to find the statue in no time on their own.

The following morning, breakfast is delivered to the common area outside their rooms. It is an incredible spread meant to make them feel at home in this foreign land. The table overflows with American fare like fluffy scrambled eggs, crispy bacon, and seasoned potatoes, as well as a delicious array of Hawaiian fruits—papaya, mango, and pineapple.

"Mol, why didn't you tell me how bad your situation was?" Hillary takes a huge bite out of a chocolate croissant.

Heidi and Moa, well out of earshot, have created a fort out of Moa's bedding and are camping out on the balcony reading the book on ancient Egypt from the newly opened bookcase.

"After Steve died, I got so depressed." Molly's eyes welled with tears. "The surf shop went under within six months and I had to close it. Steve had a sole proprietorship and all the debt fell on me. There aren't a lot of jobs on the island and I finally found a part-time job as a clerk in a gift shop. That paid for utilities and groceries."

"But I thought Steve's family owned the house." Hillary grabbed a napkin and wiped a trickle of mascara off of Molly's cheek.

"Steve's father had taken out a second mortgage and died before he could pay it off. The family was never very good with finances. Anyway, when we got the call, I thought in an odd way my prayers had been answered. The prince and his staff have been really kind to us, Hil."

"Well, we might have gotten a break." Hillary hands Molly the note.

"Why on earth would someone accidentally send a priceless statue to an import company?" Molly asks.

"Hey, Hillary, listen to this!" Moa laughs. Heidi has taught her how to make farting noises with her hand in her armpit and she is eager to share her newfound talent.

"Pleasant," Hillary says dryly.

"Know what else we found out?" Moa runs back to the tent to grab the book on ancient Egypt while Heidi fills them in on the latest she's read from the 'cool old book.'

"This book is all about when Ku lived. From what we read, it sounds like the weather might have given him trouble," Heidi says, her brow furrowing in concern. "Poor little guy."

"Now honey, I'm sure weather can be a nuisance, but it certainly can't ruin your life," Molly reasons.

"What about hurricanes? Or earthquakes...," Heidi counters.

"…or a drought," Moa adds as she returns with the book and thumbs through the pages to find the appropriate chapter, then reads:

*After the Ice Age, glaciers melted and created lush jungles in both Africa and Egypt. However, sometime around 4,000 B.C., climate change caused the once verdant jungles to dry up and become what is now the Sahara Desert. It would have been quite possible for a person during that time to witness this dramatic change in weather, firsthand. Hieroglyphs depict everyday life during that time as extremely desperate.*

*People who were otherwise civilized found themselves being forced to steal and kill just to survive.*

"Poor, Ku!" Heidi said.

"It's heartbreaking to imagine what he might have faced as a child in those circumstances." Molly shakes her head.

"How about we explore an Egyptian open-air market?" Hillary places her napkin on the table and gets up, "Maybe we'll find a clue about the statue. And who knows, perhaps we might find out a bit more about Ku."

The baby monkey began to eat out of my hand. I introduced him to Am and we marveled at how resilient he was about any harm that had come to him before. We decided to name him Meep because that was the sound he made when he saw us. After several weeks of giving him crumbs, he began to help me out in the fields. I use the term "help" loosely. What Meep would do was to pull weeds, replace them elsewhere, and take the rocks that we had cleared and throw them back into the field.

Still, all in all, he was a great source of entertainment and he became a part of our odd little family.

While we'd play, out of the corner of my eye I'd see Hap watching. Hap did very little work and quite a lot of observing. It seemed that the harder I worked, the more Hap complained. He had a way of making the work I did into something harmful or wrong. For example, I cleared too much land too quickly. That caused him to have to overuse the animals in clearing his portion of the field. Or I cleared too slowly, causing the animals to get restless and lazy. It was always something. And when Hap complained, Fet listened. Before long, I couldn't go a day without a reprimand.

Am escaped all of this because she was invisible from the start. In Fet's eyes, Am ranked a minor step above the farm animals. What was most amazing to me was that she seemed to find a pocket of serenity within her living arrangement. She went about her chores with a calm centeredness that was way beyond her years. Her demeanor reminded me of the shaman who had visited my village,

I wasn't sure what made me angrier, watching Fet ignore the beauty and peace in Am or experiencing his underhanded fury channeled through Hap. But I dared not retaliate with words or actions because he provided something I was not able to find elsewhere: food and board.

Another thing that seemed to affect everyone was the drought. It had not rained a drop since I had arrived, and that had been six months ago. Fet seemed to unravel more and more with each day that passed. Am and I felt lucky that he continued to provide food and water, and that we had Meep as a companion to break the monotony of our long work hours.

One morning, Fet awoke in an especially cantankerous mood. It was normal for him to exchange words with Hap while we worked in the field; however, on this day he threw off Hap as if he were, well, as if he were me. Hap was quite upset by this brush-off and, even from my vantage point in the fields, I could see him scheming for a way to get Fet's attention. So when Meep began his usual play version of "help," Hap ran to Fet and began to speak animatedly. A gnawing feeling began in my stomach and got worse as Hap chattered. Fet listened intently until he stood and bellowed at me to come.

I stood and dusted myself off, stretching here and there because I'd become stiff from my morning's work. In truth, I was grateful for a respite, but fearful of what was to come. As I approached, I could feel Meep at my side and when I arrived, he climbed up my leg and perched on my shoulder.

We had become close, Meep and I. He would sleep with me, work with me, and eat with me. Other than Am, he was my dearest friend.

Hap approached me with an unnerving glee. "Fet says there has been no rain and that we must perform a sacrificial ritual."

How anyone could say something like this without remorse was beyond me. My blood ran cold. I stood saying nothing, sick with fear of what would come next.

Fet pointed to Meep, clinging to my shoulder, and Hap took a step in my direction. I turned on my heel and sprinted as fast as my legs could take me toward to desert. Night after night I'd planned my escape from this place and at that moment my plan came to life. Run for the desert and survive in any way I could. Unfortunately, my plans had included food and water. I'd have to figure out another scenario. Meep was my heart and I was not about to let him be sacrificed.

We ran through brush, over rocks and through sand. But Hap ran faster and overtook me after a mile.

He wrenched Meep from my clutches and sprinted away from me back toward the desiccated farm.

I wept bitterly, letting my tears fall onto the sandy soil as I lay face down in the place on which I had been tackled and robbed of what had come to mean most to me. Meep had been a ray of hope in my terrifyingly bleak situation.

The wind picked up and the sky turned dark. At first I thought it might rain, but instead a hot dry wind blew fiercely, a sandstorm raging around me as I sought shelter between two rocks, falling into a deep, grief-stricken sleep.

When I awoke, the full moon was up and the sky was clear with twinkling stars. It was almost as if no one had witnessed the horrific incident with Meep. The failed reality of my escape sunk in. I had no supplies, no way to travel and to camp safely. So, I snuck back into my hut, not that Fet or Hap would notice or care, as they had slaughtered the very thing I'd nurtured and loved.

My mat and few belongings were as I'd left them. But nothing looked the same. Grief has a funny way of changing what our eyes see, and my eyes saw the truth: I was a slave and if I did not leave this place soon, I would die here. Tears filled my eyes as I realized my true predicament. The only way out was through the desert. And no one survived a sandy, arid journey like that.

I began to see why people stay slaves: fear. Although every human being has a choice to be free, sometimes that choice is overshadowed by the fear of death. In that moment, I gave up ever leaving that awful place and resigned myself to endlessly clearing that rocky, infertile field.

When I awoke the next morning, Fet sat in his usual spot, his withering face gnarled into a grimace. And when he saw me exit my hut to begin my work, he taunted me, "Why bother leaving? You'll only die. I have food and water. What more could you need?" The sun sent splinters of light in every direction as Fet took a long drink of his fermented frothy beer and leaned back with a smug, satisfied grin.

# CHAPTER VII
# Assault of the Senses

### Ritual: Healing the Soul
### Stone: Chalcedony
### Blend: Warrior Elixir

---

*Fill a bathtub with warm water. Add a cup of sea salt, a pinch of pepper, and a bay leaf. Stir the bath with your hand clockwise three times and say the following: "Today my soul is filled with light, love, healthy protection. May this bath bring the healing my soul needs and the sustenance my soul requires."*

*As you soak, believe that your intention for your soul-healing bath will be fulfilled.*

*Blessed Be.*

"Ew, it smells like dirty feet!" Heidi holds her nose. The group has been dropped off by a palace limousine and is standing at the entrance of one of Egypt's largest and longest-running markets. A hot breeze whips through Moa's long, brown hair and swirls up and around Molly's beautiful, hand-beaded skirt, prompting her to hold it down with both hands.

Hillary's brilliant idea of checking every stall in the market goes out the window when she sees the number of stalls. The foursome stares at row upon row, tent after tent of fabrics flapping in the wind, giving the illusion of a vast, roiling sea. The stalls are draped with colorful fabrics and the loud din gives the impression that vendors are competing for decibel levels.

Molly puts her hands over her ears, "I think I am more worried about damage to my eardrums than the stench."

"Okay." Hillary is all business. "Let's split up and meet here in one hour. Moa and I will cover as many stands to the right as we can and, Mol, you and Heidi cover the stalls to the left. When we meet back, we can compare notes."

"Sounds good to me." Molly takes Heidi's hand and says, "Stay close to me, Heidi. It's really crowded and I don't want you to get lost."

Moa and Hillary walk toward the first stall, but Moa stops. Hillary turns and looks back, "What's wrong? We're looking for the statue. Isn't that what you want?"

"Something strange is going on here. I can't tell if it is good or bad, but my stomach feels funny."

"Maybe it was something you ate?" Hillary is starting to get annoyed.

"Maybe it wasn't?" Moa squares off. Her tiny frame stiffens and she puts her hands on her hips.

Hillary wipes perspiration from her forehead and sighs. "Look. You don't have your powers any more. If you feel something, it is most likely the six chocolate macaroons you had at breakfast."

"No, it feels like a bubble, right here." Moa furrows her brow and puts her hand up to her diaphragm.

"That's indigestion." Hillary says gently, "Come on, we don't have a lot of time." Hillary puts her arm around Moa's shoulders and escorts her into the market.

Hillary and Moa approach the first stall and watch a local woman, draped from head to toe in black, barter —or argue, the language barrier makes it difficult to discern— with a salesman wearing orange linen pants and a matching tunic. Finally, the "discussion" is over and Hillary approaches hesitantly.

"H-hello, um, do you speak English?"

"Yes," the salesman nods. "A lootle Anglish."

"We are in search of a statue...of Ku..." Hillary begins.

"Mmmmm, stertooo. Koooo," the salesman ruminates.

"It is made of stone," Hillary says.

"With pink coral," Moa adds hopefully.

The salesman's face lights up, puts his index finger up asking for them to wait, and disappears behind a curtain in the stall.

"Won't it be amazing if we find the statue on our first try?" Moa says excitedly.

The salesman returns with a statue and hands it to Moa.

"This is incredible. Moa do you believe it? Our first try!" Hillary squeals. "Thank you, thank you so much!" she gushes to the grinning salesman.

Moa does not react, but silently looks the statue over.

"Moa," Hillary says, "thank the man. He found your family's statue!"

The salesman nods and smiles, happy to accommodate them. However, Moa continues to examine the statue.

"What could possibly be wrong?!" Hillary explodes. "We found your statue! It's here, in your hands. Say 'thank you' to this man for helping us!"

"It's not mine. It's way smaller than I remember," Moa says sadly. "And it's plastic. Here, look." She hands the statue to Hillary.

Hillary's expression turns dark. "Sir," she says through gritted teeth. "We are looking for a real stone statue, with actual pink coral. Do you have one?"

The man worriedly shakes his head and motions for them to follow him behind the curtain. Along the way, he mumbles, "Peeenk corale. Stertooo," and "Koooo." They arrive at a large shelving unit lined with hundreds of boxes.

He removes a lid from one of the boxes, and then another, and another. He removes twenty lids and reveals hundreds of statues of Ku.

Stunned, Hillary and Moa leave the stall and wander through stall after stall, all of which are featuring various sizes and shapes of statues of Ku. Some are plastic, others are clay. The two wearily conclude it is unlikely they will ever find Moa's family treasure this way.

At the agreed-upon time, Hillary and Moa make their way back to the entrance to meet Molly and Heidi. Hillary turns a corner and passes yet another Statue of Ku. Moa stops to look at a colorful blue-glass necklace.

"Can you believe it? All those statues but none of them was the one we want." Hillary turns back to get an answer, but Moa is nowhere to be seen. "Moa!" She screams and runs in the direction of where she last saw her sweet friend.

Months had stretched into years, three to be exact. Am and I were now both ten years old. The fields were cleared. A rockless, shadeless, weedless field stretched out to the edge of the desert. Fet continued to act as if the fields would grow vegetation, even though it had rained only twice in three years.

Fet had planned to have Am and I harvest the crops from the field we'd cleared and planted, but in his resolute delusion, he'd neglected to acknowledge a fact that was painfully obvious to everyone but him—nothing would ever grow on his land. No amount of clearing, planting, or work would change that truth.

In a moment of crazed desperation, Fet had—through Hap—ordered us to water the nonemerging seedlings ourselves. It was ghastly work. Am, Hap, and I trudged through the thorny brush to the only source of water, which was a half-day's walk away. Each one of us had to fill and transport three large, oiled animal hide sacks back to the farm. Then, Am and I were given the task of pouring water on each mound of sandy arid earth. Even though the seeds had been carefully planted in these mounds so many weeks ago and should have sprouted by now, Fet was convinced all they needed was more water.

After two weeks of constant toil, Am collapsed, and Hap and I carried her into her hut where she lay on her pallet, moaning, while I went back out into the field. I'm not sure how I managed alone, but I did. Still, I worried about Am almost constantly.

One evening, I snuck into her hut to see how she was recovering. The hut was mud with clay and grass walls, like mine, but with a warm loving touch in the decor. She had collections of beautiful rocks, some of which she'd tumbled with sand until they were polished.

She did not look at all well. Her face was gray green and her lips were as dry and cracked as the broken earth. I dipped a gourd, which was in a bucket filled with water, and put it to her lips.

"Ku, you must leave here." The words escaped Am's mouth in a harsh whisper.

"No one has ever escaped into the desert and I cannot go back the way I came." I brushed the hair out of her eyes. "Fet is right. I should not bother. And at least you and I have each other."

"No!" Am's determined tone was infused with a parental thread. "You are meant for more than this."

"As are you..."

"Listen to me, Ku." She grabbed my hand and directed her glassy eyes into mine. "Fet is using fear to control you. You can either let fear control you or let it go. The choice is up to you."

I sat with that statement for a minute. She was right. I had the freedom to choose.

She continued with renewed strength. "Meep was sacrificed. Who knows who could be next?"

"We'll leave together. I will bring enough food for us both."

"I am not meant to go. But you are. I will help you to escape by gathering the provisions which will sustain you to your next location."

"I'm not leaving without you." A shudder ran through me as I tried to imagine going out alone and leaving my friend.

"If anyone can do this, Ku, it is you. I gathered some food—enough for two weeks—and found a special gourd, which will carry water. If you are careful with your supplies, you can survive in the desert."

She pointed to a rock in the corner of her hut and asked me to lift it up. When I did, I saw a hole. Inside was a braided grass mat, which had been fashioned into a sack.

I left the mat untouched, replaced the rock and moved back up toward Am. "I'm not leaving you."

"You must! I promise I will think every day of our time together, your stories, and of Meep." She took another gulp of water from the gourd, "You must promise me that you will do the same. Trust me, Ku, when I say that things will never get better here. Your only chance for survival is to leave. Fet has it in for you, he means to harm you when the time is right. He seeks vengeance against your family for a feud fought long before you were born but which still festers. Look beneath the braided mat back under the rock."

I again removed the rock and picked up the bag. Below it were two silver pieces with stamps on each side. They were my family's insignia—three parallel wavy lines—meant to signify water. At once, I felt like I was back in my old village, at my father's side. He was telling my brothers and me the legacy of these mystical medallions. Each one was made by my great grandfather and saved through the years. My father carried one medallion with him and said that there were two others. Legend had it that my grandfather's best friend stole the remaining coins. This egregious act created a feud that lasted through generations.

"Where did you get these?" Am avoided my gaze. I continued, "I am not those people who came before me." I picked up a dirt clod and rolled it between my forefinger and thumb. "A cruel monster stole my healing gifts." A small cloud of dust exploded from my fingers as I crushed the clod. "I am merely a person now."

Unwilling to accept my pain, she continued, "If you die in this place, thousands will perish. As long as you have a breath of life within you, you can make a difference in this world, Ku. I cannot tell you how I know this, I just do." She paused and let her words sink in. "Fet is not of right mind and he has Hap to help with the physical chores. He will make you suffer. I cannot allow that. Here's what you will do. Tomorrow morning when Fet comes out to deliver our new set of daily chores, I will get Hap to come into my tent. Pack your sack tonight and have it ready and when Hap is distracted, you can slip away."

I nodded but at the time had no intention of leaving without her. We did not speak further. I sat with her until she fell asleep, then I crept out of her hut and back into mine, where I sat thinking of the effort it must have taken for Am to collect the provisions for me. She had also taken a terrible risk by stealing the metal medallions from Fet. Surely he'd find them missing and then Fet would go after Am. I resolved to take her with me, no matter what she said.

I barely slept that night and when I awoke, it was before dawn. I carefully gathered my belongings, rolled my mat, put my pelt into my father's hunting sack and said a silent good-bye to Meep's spirit.

As the sun rose, however, something was definitely different. For whatever reason, the sunlight had a filtered quality. Although Fet was his surly self, Hap was strangely energized. *Did Hap know about our escape plan?*

Am did not come out of her hut. I thought about going in to check on her, when I heard yelling from within its confines. Well, it was not as much yelling, as it was yelping—a high-pitched, piercing yodel of a yelp all coming from Hap. He emerged from the hut with blood trickling down his ear yodeling about Am. She came out looking much improved, with a triumphant sparkle in her eye. While Hap relayed to Fet that the cause of his injury was Am, I quickly pulled Am into her hut.

"You see!" she said, greeting me with a smile. "It's time for you to go. Now grab the sack and leave."

"You're coming with me," I said stubbornly.

But I was interrupted by a crash upon my head from behind.

When I next awoke it was predawn. My wrists and ankles were tied in front of me and I was gagged with fabric, which had been knotted into a ball. My head was pulsating and my right eye was swollen shut. Through my left eye, I could make out the faint outline of a large snoring blob. I was in Fet's house. It was anyone's guess how long I'd been lying on his floor.

I could hear crying outside and then voices shouting. Perhaps Hap and Am were arguing. Then, I heard a loud crash, followed by thumping steps in my direction. *Was Hap coming back to finish me off?* I braced myself for the worst.

CHAPTER VIII

# Here by Choice…and by Sacrifice

## Ritual: Ancient Contract Retrieval
## Stone: Elestial Quartz
## Blend: Exhale Elixir

*At midnight on a new moon, spray the elixir in a circle inside which you will sit. Believe you are protected within your space and write down a problem you wish to solve on a small piece of paper. Breathe in the new moon energy and know that all that you need to know will be revealed in this ritual. Hold the piece of paper in your left hand and ask to see the Ancient Contract, which binds you to this problem in your right hand. In your mind's eye, see a piece of paper appear. Then imagine that a title appears at the top of the page. Then see the names and/or faces of those who are/were connected either in this lifetime or in past lifetimes to the problem*

*you've written. What does your list look like? Are there more names than you thought there would be? Fewer names than you expected? Many people go lifetimes with contracts just like this. It is your choice whether or not you continue on with your Ancient Contract in its current state.*

*Blessed Be.*

illary frantically races around the area in which she last saw Moa, retracing her steps, looking into booths, behind tents, calling out her name. Finally she pushes through the booth next to the last place she saw Moa. There she counters a male shopkeeper's blank stare with a frustrated scream, "She has to be here!" But upon discovering that her friend is not behind the tent flaps of a rug stall, Hillary tearfully pleads with the confused looking gnomelike stall owner, "Her name is Moa. She's a little girl, with dark hair. She just has to be here."

In her panic, Hillary decides to go back to the entrance to see if Moa might have gone on ahead. There she meets up with Molly and Heidi and shares the distressing news.

"She doesn't have her special powers!" Hillary wails, breaking down in Molly's arms. "What will she do without them?"

Heidi stands next to her mother and rubs Hillary's back. "Aunt Hillary, this is Moa's first test in her new human body."

"Sweetheart, I feel responsible for Moa." Hillary tries to hold it together and turns to Molly. "The last time I saw Moa, she was looking in the direction of some jewelry."

"But, Aunt Hillary," Heidi interrupts, "if this is her test, maybe it's ours, too. We might have to try to be more like Moa was and use our own special gifts to find her."

Molly and Hillary stop talking and look at Heidi.

"You know what?" Hillary kneels down to Heidi's level so that she is eye to eye with her niece. "You're right."

"Well, I'm not sure how I can help," Molly throws her hands up in the air. "I don't have any gifts."

"Don't you remember what Moa said, Mom? She said that words are extremely powerful. If you say 'I don't have any gifts,' your words will come true! You will never see your gifts. But, if you do want to see them and discover them, then all you need to do is to change those words."

Molly shifts uncomfortably and looks around, "Sure. Fine. I have gifts. But, the more time we spend talking, the farther away Moa could be getting. Let's walk and talk."

They walk together back into the crowded market.

"Is it possible that there are even more people here than just ten minutes ago? Stay with me," Hillary yells back to Molly and Heidi, as she squeezes through a tightly packed pocket of people bargaining for fresh melons.

Hillary makes her way back to the spot where she last saw Moa, Molly, and Heidi in tow. When the three finally find a space large enough for them to gather, Hillary says, "It is such a long shot that she'd be anywhere near here, but I keep being drawn back to this spot."

Heidi pipes up, "Well, maybe that's your gift. Perhaps some part of you knows where Moa is, but your mind doesn't."

"Well," Hillary yells to be heard over the din, "Heidi, you mentioned that Moa said that words are powerful. What about thoughts?" Two men transporting a large crate yell at the crowd to get them to part, interrupting Hillary. Once they've passed, Hillary continues, "Moa said that positive emotions are higher and negative emotions are lower, and that you can lock in a vibration with carefully chosen words." Hillary gets jostled by a large woman carrying several baskets laden with fruits and vegetables and shoots a stern glance in the woman's direction as she gives a frustrated sigh. "I feel like I'm trying to stand my ground in a rough ocean." She smiles slightly. "We are all faced with little annoyances, like the people knocking me around while I was trying to talk. Just like I found a way to stay positive, I think if we think about Moa and concentrate on believing she is safe and still in the market, perhaps we'll find her."

"It can't hurt," Molly says uncomfortably. Two extremely tall people have their backs to her and are pressed against her and are speaking animatedly.

"Okay," Hillary takes Heidi's hand, "I know she's in one of these tents…"

Hillary takes two steps forward but a young man carrying a sack of grain knocks her shoulder and sends her stumbling into a table covered with colorful bottles filled with oils and sprays. They fly everywhere!

"Oh," Hillary begins to pick up the glass. "I am so sorry!" She says to the stall's owner, a smartly dressed petite, young woman. "Let me help," Hillary says, frowning at the back of the young man who scurries away with his sack.

Meanwhile, Moa wanders up and down the stalls yelling for Hillary to no avail. She decides that perhaps she should just look for the Statue of Ku herself and then find Hillary, Molly, and Heidi. Her first stop is an old sage who is selling mystical readings. He wears a white turban and a gray robe and sits in the lotus position with his eyes closed.

"Excuse me sir," Moa says politely. "I am looking for the Statue of Ku."

The man opens his eyes and nods. "Yes, Ku." He speaks English very well. "But people pay good money for my help. What can you offer me if I help you?"

Moa thinks for a moment, then declares, "I have no money, but perhaps your finding the statue has more value in the search."

The man laughs. "You are a wise one. It is true that there is value in a search. But telling people their fortunes is my livelihood."

"Well," Moa says coyly, "What if I could promise you a wonderful feast at the end of our search?"

"My, you *are* a special one, aren't you? Here by choice... and by sacrifice." The man closes his eyes once more and hums. Then, in a high squeaky voice he says, "The statue will find you."

Moa shifts from one foot to another waiting for the old man's crinkly eyes to open. "Excuse me," she whispers quietly. But he is deep in meditation.


Hillary untangles herself from the tablecloth covering the table she has upended. Molly pulls her up and Heidi tries to gather as many fallen bottles as possible.

"I'm so sorry," Hillary says to a kind-looking woman who has rushed to help her up as well.

"It is okay." The smartly dressed woman wears a beautiful red sari with gold thread woven throughout. "Are you hurt?"

"Um...I don't think so." Hillary dusts herself off. Then she reaches down to pick up the table. "I'm Hillary, this is Molly and Heidi. "We're searching for..."

Heidi interrupts. "We're looking for Moa. The prince said we could look wherever we want to..." Then she walks, unnoticed, toward the back of the tent while Hillary and Molly continue.

"Our little one is so special," Molly says, close to tears, "If you'll just let us take a look around…"

"Hey, Mom, there are a whole bunch of babies back here! One, two, three…" Heidi is now at the back of the stall with her head poked behind the tent flap.

The woman runs toward Heidi, then seems to recover quickly. "I am Geti. You have cut yourself and I will help you dress your wound. Please come rest and have some tea with my family in our back lounge area."

Hillary looks down to examine a cut on her right palm. It's not deep, but she could use a Band-Aid. "I was so distracted, I didn't see it." Half curious about what Heidi saw behind the stall, Hillary follows Geti and Molly to the back of the tent.

Geti pulls open a flap in the back of the tent and motions for Heidi, Hillary, and Molly to enter. The three let their eyes adjust to the dim light and then gasp simultaneously. A large white delivery van with no windows sits with its back doors open, and eight babies in car carriers are lined up.

"Oh, this cannot be good." Hillary looks around for an escape route, but tent fabric surrounds the area.

"Mommy, why does she have so many babies?" Heidi pulls on Molly's sleeve.

"We really must get on with our search." Hillary tries to exit back through the stall.

Geti blocks her way, "You're not going anywhere." She raises her hand up and pulls a chain. Within seconds, metal grating, which is normally used to lock the stalls up at night, rolls down. Geti slams the van's doors shut, then bangs on them to signal the driver, who pulls away. Then she yanks the last chain and the final grate falls. The foursome is surrounded by metal grating, a dusty dirt floor, and a chain-link ceiling, which is covered by nailed wood planks.

A little light shines through the slats in the wooden ceiling, but otherwise, it is dark. They hear Geti's footsteps fade into the muffled din of the market. However, as her eyes adjust, Molly spies some blankets in a pile next to some crates.

"I'm scared, Mom. Why did she have so many babies?" Heidi stays close to Molly as she pulls out a few and spreads them on the earth floor.

"Sweetie, she was delivering the babies somewhere, we're just not sure where." Molly does her best to soothe Heidi's fears.

Hillary's eyes are adjusting and she feels around the grating for any latches or locks.

"We certainly stumbled upon a…OW!" Hillary lets out a yelp and holds her foot.

A piercing wail brings them all to their feet and scrambling toward Hillary.

"Is that what I think it is?" Hillary pulls at a carrier that has been wedged behind two large packing crates and places it into a sliver of light.

"Oh my God!" Molly lurches toward the shaking baby carrier, "It's a baby!"

The thick grass rope that Hap had used to tie me up was digging into my wrists and ankles. I looked over at Fet, who lay in the next room and continued to snore loudly. Surprisingly, he had slept through the loud crash which had occurred during Am's and Hap's argument. All was quiet, except for an occasional wet snortle from Fet.

Suddenly, Am appeared at my side. She carried the braided sack she'd carefully prepared for me, as well as my sack with my personal belongings. Setting them down, she produced a knife from her sack and carefully cut the rope tethering my wrists and ankles, which I rubbed to get the blood flowing freely, as Am whispered instructions. I watched as her elegant long fingers pulled at the rope. Her soft, kind eyes had a slight twinkle as she handed me the sacks. She had grown into a lovely girl.

"Take these to the giant rock at the far edge of the desert. You know the one you hid in for shelter during the sandstorm? I will meet you there, Ku."

"Seems as if Fet can sleep through anything!" I laughed.

"I placed a special sleep herb in his drink last night. He'll sleep for a while." Am shoved the two sacks into my hands.

"What about Hap?" I asked as she pushed me out of the hut.

"I cracked him on the head with a pot. He's out now. Who knows when he'll come to, but when he does, he'll be angry." She opened her hand and revealed one of her beautiful, hand-polished stones. It sparkled with flecks of green, purple, pink, and yellow. "Take this, Ku. It is a very special stone and will protect you from that awful monster that stole your gifts and from anyone else who would dare try to harm you. Keep it with you always."

"Am, are you sure you will meet me?" I knew I must go to save myself but was worried about Am.

"I will join you as soon as I am able." Her hand was out, offering me the gorgeous stone; it was obvious that she desperately wanted me to have it.

Hap moaned as he began to come back to consciousness.

"But what if you can't get away?" I whispered.

"Ku." Am's eyes darted to Fet and then back to me. "Fet was your grandfather's enemy. I stole those coins from him so you would have proof. I promise I'll meet you at our appointed spot. Now go!"

I took the sacks, one in each hand—ignoring the stone in her outstretched hand— then turned to run toward our appointed meeting location, yelling over my shoulder. "You can bring the stone with you."

I ran away, firmly believing that Am would join me soon.

The spot Am had chosen for us to meet was ingenious. From the outside, it looked like a pile of smallish stones, with a small opening for a small animal. The front stone was loose, however, and if removed gave access to a roomy space—big enough for both of us to sit. Inside it was cramped but comfortable. Once I'd settled in to my hiding place, I went through the bag that Am had lovingly prepared. It contained several smaller braided bags which contained nourishing *tongan* root, betel nuts, dried *moni* berries, and several gourds filled to the brim with water. The most astonishing thing about the package was the amounts of these items that Am had managed to amass. As she'd indicated before, there were indeed enough provisions for two weeks of sustenance.

At sunset, I still had not seen or heard from Am and was doing my best to keep up hope that she would soon be with me. I slept with one eye and one ear open, trying to discern between the howling of the wind and any whisper that might be from Am. Finally, I heard the distinctive snap and crunch of earth and sand and knew that she was coming. Something kept me from moving from my spot, however. If it was Am, she knew exactly where I'd tucked myself away and would find me. No need to risk my own demise. As the person approached, I sadly noted that the sound of the steps was heavier than Am's. My heart fell as I realized it must be Hap, and judging from the short huffing sound, it seemed he was not happy about having to search for me so late at night. Then I heard a plop right in front of the entrance. Hap had apparently planted himself right in front of my only means of escape.

Crouched here in my protective spot brought back the memory of the cave in my family's village. It seemed almost a lifetime ago that I'd made the devastating discovery about my family and had to flee so quickly. My stomach churned as I imagined what might have happened to Am, and I decided I'd rather be back with her, even if it meant sacrificing my freedom. I pushed against the stone blocking the entrance and felt the heaviness of a body against it. So, I pushed harder. There was no need to worry about making a disturbance since I was going to show myself. I shoved the stone as hard as I could and managed to move it and whatever part of my pursuer's body was blocking it.

When I emerged from the place, I was stunned to see Am instead of Hap. The knife she'd used to cut my ligatures protruded from her lower chest, and blood covered the lower half of her body. Who knows what she'd endured to get here? The life had almost drained from her still body, and her skin was an eerie pale gray.

I let out a scream, not caring who or what could hear me, and roared with the agony that comes from compounded loss. Grief for my parents, brothers, and little sister, grief from the cruelty to my beloved Meep, and now grief for my dear friend, Am, poured from me as I grabbed at Am's body and pleaded with the gods, the angels, my guides, anyone who could hear me to return my healing powers.

Her eyes fluttered. She was alive. I pressed my ear against her mouth as she gurgled, "Stone...take it." Then she was gone. It caught the light of the moon that sparkled between her slim fingers, despite the blood spatter. The stone! Her tiny hand clutched it tightly and it took some effort to pry it out. Once I did, I put it to my heart. A wash of calm entered my body. This stone was truly special.

Pressing my lips to her forehead, I whispered, "Am, I love you. Thank you for my stone. I will treasure it always." The breeze caught her long hair and, for a moment, I thought she might still be alive. But she was not. My heart sank further into my stomach as I crawled back into the space, retrieved the two bags, and made my way to the desert.

As I did so, I held the stone tightly in my hand and imagined all that Am had to endure to deliver that stone. If I was meant to die, so be it. Am's voice echoed in my head as I took my first steps toward an uncertain future: "You can either let fear control you or let it go. The choice is up to you."

CHAPTER IX

# Apep is Near

Ritual: Ancient Contract Termination
Stone: Elestial Quartz
Blend: Cord-severing Elixir

---

*Remain seated with the problem you've written on the scrap of paper in your left hand. As you sit quietly seeing the Ancient Contract, which has appeared in your right hand, know that you have two choices. You may do nothing and keep the Ancient Contract as is, or you can sever the Contract. If you wish to keep the Contract as is, read no further. This ritual is for those who wish to sever the Ancient Contract and walk a new path.*
*By choosing to sever your Ancient Contract, you agree to release any and all behaviors, patterns, and feelings as well as any past associations with them, such as shame, guilt, and blame, either for yourself or anyone else. The ritual makes your Ancient Contract null and void.*

*Do not attempt this ritual until you can fully commit to terminating your Ancient Contract. Bring your awareness to your Ancient Contract in your right hand. What feelings does it evoke? Memories? Imagine a cord, which is connected to the Contract and is attached to a part of your body. Where does it lead? Your head? Your pelvis? Heart? Say the following:*

*I release the cord that binds me.*
*No longer, will I follow blindly.*
*Begin again.*
*With senses refreshed*
*No longer enmeshed*
*I am free to proceed as my will guides me.*

*If you happen to experience or sense any behaviors, patterns, or feelings that you connect with the old Contract, know that you have done your part in releasing the past and are free to move forward with confidence.*

*Blessed Be.*

Molly runs the back of her hand across the baby's mocha, satiny-soft checks and coos into his beautiful, almond-shaped, dark-brown eyes. She thoroughly checks his arms, legs, and torso to make sure he is not hurt. "He looks like he's about five months old," she finally announces "and he's got a wet diaper."

"Well, surely they will figure out this baby is missing and then we'll be in big trouble. We have got to get out of here." Hillary runs her hands along the bars to see if there is any other way to escape. She holds up a piece of thick metal pipe uncovered from a crate near the baby's carrier and tries in vain to pry the grating away from its track, then hits at the grating in frustration. She lets the pipe fall with a loud clank. "How on earth are we going to find Moa now?"

The baby falls asleep and Molly gently places him back in the carrier.

"Hey," Heidi puts her hand on Hillary's hand. "What if, instead of trying to find Moa, we get her to find us?"

"But Moa doesn't have her extrasensory powers, love." Molly puts her hand on Heidi's shoulder.

"I know, Mom." Heidi resolutely says, "But we have to try something!"

"Alright, let's all sit and think happy thoughts about Moa." Hillary shifts around trying to get comfortable on the blanket.

"I think we might need to do more than that," Heidi says. "I believe Moa is close by. In fact, I'm sure she will find us."

"She's probably headed our way right now," Molly says, catching on.

"Is she walking from aisle to aisle, asking about us?" Hillary asks hopefully. "I can see her...okay." She pauses, then sighs with frustration. "This is ridiculous, you guys..."

"Keep going, Hil," Molly encourages.

"I just got a mental picture and I 'see' her sitting on the moon," Hillary says glumly. "I think I just flunked the test."

Moa is tired from her search for Hillary, Heidi, and Molly and perches on a round marble statue.

"Little girl," says an annoyed disheveled male artist. "You must get off my moon!"

Moa hops off and peruses the stall's wares. Sure enough, she has been seated on a beautiful black marble lunar replica.

"Where are your parents?" The artist runs his fingers through his wiry, black hair.

"In the realm of the Light." Moa moves her hands across a lovely granite obelisk.

This time the man squeezes between Moa and the sculpture and points toward the exit. "I think I hear them calling you."

Moa sees some children playing with a balloon and follows them. They disappear between two stalls. She peeks through, then decides to go after them.

The children are playing in a large, open space surrounded by the backs of tents. Half a dozen women sit on folding chairs, talking. Burning incense covers the comingling aromas of broiling meat and rotting vegetables. The children scream and laugh as they bat a blue balloon around. A loud pop ends the game and they begin a raucous game of tag.

"Excuse me?" Moa asks one of the women in the group, a tiny woman with a blue-and-silver sari.

She looks up and gives her a kind nod. "What is it, little one?"

"I'm looking for my friends—two women and a girl about my age. Have you seen them?"

She motions for Moa to sit on a small brocade ottoman next to her. "My name is Endo. What is your name?"

"Moa."

There is a flurry as the women speak in their native tongue. Endo rises, takes Moa's hand and leads her back into the market. They search until it is nearly dark, and with Endo as the translator, they manage to cover more ground than Moa did before.

"I'm so sorry, Moa." Endo, barely a head taller than Moa, sadly shakes her head. "No one has seen your friends. It is almost dark. Come back with me and we will rest before we search again. We will find them, I promise."

The two head back to the rest area. As Moa and Endo approach the group of women, someone produces, as if from thin air, a beautiful china teacup and saucer filled with an aromatic blend of tea.

A willowy woman in red moves another tufted ottoman across from Moa and sets down the tea and a small bowl containing an aromatic stew. She stands back and watches with curiosity while Moa sips from the teacup.

Moa guesses the ingredients aloud as she draws the beautiful scent far into her nostrils, "Mmmm, rosemary, cinnamon, sage and…" she tries to discern the last one. "It's not a spice, it's an herb…is that thyme?"

The women titter and giggle. The woman in red says, "Hello, dear one. My name is Semi. You are right about the ingredients. How did you become so good at guessing herbs and spices?"

Moa puts her hand up to her reddening cheek. "I, uh, haven't been here very long, but I have an extensive background in herbal remedies. My mother taught me all that she knew."

Endo smiles. "You are quite articulate for one of your age."

Moa nods. "I really need to find my friends."

Endo gives her a hug. "Before we begin our search again, can we try something? It is an ancient ritual that, I believe, might help you to find your friends."

"Okay." Moa shrugs.

"First," Endo takes her hand, "you must clear yourself. To do this, you must think of one good thing you have done. Imagine that it becomes a lovely green light in your chest.

Then imagine the light growing beyond your chest and surrounding you with a loving aura."

Moa puts her hand on chest, "I feel a vibrating. That's my self, saying it's okay to be who I am."

"Yes, it is!" Endo says encouragingly. "Now, you must clear your surroundings." Endo takes an ornate glass spray bottle from a pocket in her skirt and walks around the small tent, spritzing the air around herself and Moa.

"What is that?" Moa points to the spray.

"It is a gem elixir." Endo continues to move around in a circle, creating a wider and wider berth around Moa. "If you'd like, I can show you and your friends how to make them."

"I'd like that." Moa relaxes.

"Imagine that you are using your hands to sweep up any negative energy." She ends up at the space between the tents, and with one large sweeping motion, sends all the gathered energy up into the sky.

"I feel it!" Moa squeals. "The tent feels crisp and clean, like the air was filtered."

"Now." Endo stows the elixir spray back into her skirt pocket. "Where are your friends?"

"I don't know!" Moa dashes for the exit, "I have to get out of here."

"Where are we going?" Endo quickly follows.

"I don't know…I feel trapped…"

During my stay at Fet's compound, the desert had virtually taken over his land. Drifting sand had overtaken the rock on which I'd sat and first seen Fet, and as I approached it again, I remembered my terror of the desert. As I stood in the same place, three years later, ready to embark on a new journey, I saw my fear in a new way. The fact that no one had made it through the desert before presented a challenge, but I believed that my thoughts would help me to stay alive.

I tried to take stock of the good in my situation. I had food, water, and something I'd never thought was important before—I had freedom. As I hiked, I tried to imagine what kind of people, if any, could survive in this harsh climate. About halfway through the first day, the terrain changed from sandy clay soil to all sand. As I walked, my feet shifted and sank, making walking more challenging. The sacks stuck to my back in the heat and I longed for shade.

That first evening, I watched the full moon rise over the desert horizon. The higher it got, the more it created glowing, glittering pockets as it reflected off of the sand. The effect was an image of hundreds of shimmering miniature lakes and toward the horizon, what looked like an ocean. As

I drifted off to sleep that night, I vowed to try to make this my home, if I could figure out a way to survive its harshness.

CAW!

I was awakened in the predawn by a large, curious buzzard, which obviously, had not encountered many humans. She squawked and cawed at me, so much so that I thought I might be sitting on a nest. Since I was up, I gathered my bags and began my day's walking. Luckily, I had the full moon for light and the coolness to go with it.

As the sun rose, sweat began to trickle down my back, but I continued on. At the height of the sun, I managed to find a large indentation in a dune, which had boulders on its underside. The result was a pocket of shade, with enough space for my body to fit. I began my journey again, until I was too tired to go on. This, I surmised, was the best way to move through the desert: early morning travel, rest at midday, and then traveling in the late afternoon hours until dusk.

I had managed to mete out my supplies and eked out two and a half weeks of food and water, but seemed to be no closer to water or vegetation than when I first began. The buzzard—I named her Apep, the personification of evil—had followed me for those two weeks. I'd watched as she circled and cawed at me during my arduous trek. It occurred to me that Apep actually had seen humans before, but most likely not in my current state. Fear began to creep back into my soul as I continued my scheduled walks. However, the new moon made traveling through pitch-black desert almost impossible and I had to cut the timing down to accommodate the shifting light.

During my walks, I'd often talk with my father. Even if I couldn't hear him, surely he could hear me and, perhaps, he could help me get through this hellish trip. I never directly addressed Apep, but she appeared at some of the darkest parts of my journey and continued to hover just on the periphery.

My bags were almost empty, except for the grass mat, empty water gourds, and Am's glittering stone. I had figured out a way to walk efficiently on the sand, so I moved much more quickly. This type of travel tired me out more rapidly, however, and I decided to rest next to a large boulder with a sliver of shade. As I rounded the far side of the boulder, I reeled back in horror. There before me was a man-sized skeleton. Apep alit on the boulder and cawed loudly. Then a bit of metal caught my eye. Next to the skeleton's foot was a metal handle protruding from the sand. When I pulled it out, I was shocked to discover a metal cup bearing Fet's stamp. I ran my index finger over the X and around the slithering snake intertwined the letter.

"So," I said to the ugly, bumpy buzzard. "You think that'll be me? Are you waiting for my death?" Throwing the metal cup down, I grabbed my bags, and despite my exhaustion continued on, leaving behind the skeletal remains of Fet's former slave.

Finally, I succumbed to the light, heat, and dehydration. I tripped, fell, and lay in the same spot. Apep circled above my head as I drifted in and out of consciousness. I wondered if the end was near.

# CHAPTER X

# The Empath

## Ritual: Energetic Healing
## Stone: Selenite
## Blend: Primordial Element Elixir

*Stand with your hands together, in prayer position, at your heart.*
*Breathe in calming, cleansing light.*

*Blessed Be.*

"**G**et me out of here!" Moa screams.

Endo follows as closely as she can, but Moa is young and agile and she pulls ahead.

Finally, Moa stops, panting. Tears have made jagged streaks on her precious dusty cheeks. "I can't get out!"

She leans against a tent pole and lets out a loud wail. "HELLLLPPPP!"

Endo catches up, "Moa, maybe these feelings are not your own? Perhaps they are a clue to your friends' location. Tell me more about what you feel."

Moa hiccups, "It's hot. And I'm scared. I'm angry that I haven't found the Statue of Ku."

"Have you been worried about your safety before this?"

"No." Moa closes her eyes. "But Hillary has! It's Hillary! She is worried about me and wants to find me. She is trapped!"

"It is important that you understand that these feelings are not you. Take a deep breath, Moa," Endo soothes.

"But my heart is pounding. It is MY heart that is pounding!" Moa fixes her eyes on Endo's, desperate for comfort.

"Yes, it is true that your heart is pounding, but it is picking up the signals that another heart is sending. Kind of like an instant message." Endo sees that Moa is beginning to calm down. "Your body is receiving an emotion that someone else is sending and you are sensing it in your body."

"Okay." Moa calms slightly. "So, how do I search for my friends and not get frightened out of my wits every time an emotional message is sent?"

"Breathe," Endo instructs. "Feel the air entering your nose, passing through your throat and into your own lungs. Stamp your feet on the ground and feel them connect with the earth. Now let's press on with our search."

Back in their dimly lit musty prison, Hillary, Molly, and Heidi have reached a breaking point. No amount of positive thinking has brought Moa to them. So they have resorted to screaming and yelling for help. The baby joins them; his face turns bright red and his body shakes.

Molly can't bear to see his arms flailing in terror and picks him up, cuddles him close to her chest, and cups her hands over his tiny ears. She kisses the top of his head and hums so he can feel the vibration from her chest. Heidi hollers in the direction of where the van had been, and Hillary moves around the area and yells at the top of her lungs. Sadly, no one comes and Molly is the first to throw her hands up in defeat and collapse into the blankets. Soon Heidi joins Molly on the blanket and Hillary plops down across from her.

"We're in a market crammed with people," Molly says hoarsely, jiggling the baby in her lap to soothe him. "You'd think at least one person would have responded to our calls."

"Not even to come investigate…," Hillary coughs. She is beginning to get hoarse, as well.

Heidi puts her head on her mother's shoulder and closes her eyes.

Hillary closes her eyes, as well. Suddenly she opens them and sits up. "Moa is standing next to a tent post and she's crying."

"That doesn't sound like Moa." Molly repositions the baby so that his head is cradled in the crook of her arm.

"She's so sad." Heidi's eyes are still closed. "And she's screaming like we were."

"How do you know that, Heidi?" Molly asks.

"I can hear it. The sound is inside my head." Heidi opens her eyes wide and looks at Molly.

Molly gazes down at the baby, "Oh, keiki. I wish I knew who your parents are…were…" She drifts off into thought, then looks as if she's been struck by lightning. "Moa is feeling what we're feeling. A kind woman is with her and is helping her to find us."

Hillary and Heidi stare at Molly.

"This is new…" Hillary finally says.

"I can't explain it, but it was as if I had a thought and the thought was, 'Moa is feeling what we're feeling.'" Molly squirms in the blanket trying to get comfortable with the information. She nestles the baby back into the carrier and in an attempt to turn the attention to someone else says, "Look, if you can see her, Hil, maybe you can figure out where she is and we will be able to find her…once we escape, that is…"

"The only problem is, I don't know anything about this market, and can only see her, like in a close-up shot of a movie." Hillary shrugs.

The group processes Hillary's last thought.

Finally Heidi says, "There's got to be a way we can work together to locate Moa."

"You're right," Molly says. "But first we have to figure out how to get out of here."

Endo and Moa scour the area behind the stalls to no avail.

"It's no use," Moa says after a scruffy-looking maintenance man shakes his head when asked if he's seen her missing friends.

"Let's go back to our rest area." Endo puts her hand on Moa's back and escorts her down a less-crowded aisle. "I'll take over looking for them and then come back for you if I see anything worthwhile."

Moa nods. Her face looks different: drawn and sad. It's as if the empathic weight of others' emotions is pressing on her head and shoulders. Once in the confines of the back area, Moa opens up to Endo. "This is the hardest part about being human."

"In what form were you before?" Endo asks calmly.

"I was an Ancient Gatekeeper but chose to become human." Moa speaks quietly. "This part about the emotions is the pits!"

Endo smiles, "Yes. Yes, it is. Precious. Please take care with whom you speak about your current status. There are some who are not fans of Ancient wisdom."

"Are you?" Moa asks hopefully.

"I am." Endo smiles and pats Moa's head. "Now go play with the children. I'll be back if I find anything."

Moa walks over to a group of children who are playing a game with rocks. A circle has been drawn in the earth and they are taking turns throwing in groups of rocks.

"I'm Leti." A beautiful little girl with jet-black hair and sparkling eyes asks, "You are an Ancient aren't you?"

Moa looks around to make sure no one else hears and whispers, "Shhh. Don't say that too loud. I've learned that some people don't like Ancient wisdom."

"Well, I do." She smiles and takes Moa's hand. "Come over here. Let me show you something."

Leti wraps her soft, small hand around Moa's arm and gives a yank. Moa resists, unsure of what Leti has in mind.

"My intentions are for good. I give you my word." Leti smiles warmly.

In her current emotionally drained state, Moa decides to trust Leti's good intentions and with a weary nod, she follows Leti to a dark corner in back of one of the tents. Leti tucks her hand into a fold in the tent's flap and opens her fist to reveal a tiny box. It seems to reflect the diffused light from across the tent and sparkles brightly.

"What is it?" Moa exhales. Her stomach does a flip-flop and cartwheels.

"You know what it is." Leti smiles slyly. "This is the reason you came to Egypt."

"The Statue of Ku could not possibly be that small. I remember…"

"You are seeking more than a statue. Open it."

The box's spring creaks as Moa opens the lid.

I waited to die in the desert. Apep would occasionally swoop down to take a closer look, but when I'd open my eyes wide, the only thing I was capable of doing, she would shoot off and leave me alone. Eventually, Apep would return. As night came, I saw firelight bobbing and moving around the dunes. In my delirium, I envisioned Osiris, the god of the dead, was coming with his minions to escort me to the underworld.

Overwhelming exhaustion precluded any grief I might have felt, and I closed my eyes and waited for the light to fill my soul and to finally see my father. Instead, I heard the chatter of voices and opened my eyes to see three small men with torches surrounding me.

One pulled me up by the arm and slung me over his shoulder like a sack. The other took my bags and the third handed me a water gourd, which I drank from heartily as I bounced along. The men sang songs and hummed, but no one spoke with each other or with me.

Even though I could barely move, my heart soared inside my chest. I was saved! The men trudged along, their feet squeaking through the sand in the jet-black night, their fires lighting only our immediate area. They passed the time by chanting a singsong tune.

*Ma na na na.*
*Hezzi na. Ma na na.*

*Re ku se.*
*O se re ku se.*
*Ma na na.*

Sated with water, I was lulled into a comforting twilight sleep. Then I was awakened by an amazing sight. For a moment, I thought my eyes were playing tricks on me because I spied a leaf, then another. The men laid me down on a bed of leaves and I was finally able to see, with the help of the torches, the source of the leaves. It was a lush, green oasis! I had heard about these places from my father.

Another man handed me more water, of which I drank heartily, and then fell into a deep sleep.

I awoke in the morning to a kind woman stroking my hair. She was wiping my forehead, cheeks, and chin with water mixed with fragrant oil. When I opened my eyes, she put the leaf down and handed me a large stone plate with fresh berries, luscious flower petals, and nourishing roots. I ate quickly, smiling at her—and at the growing crowd of men, women, and children, which was gathering—between bites. I noticed that my two bags thoughtfully had been laid next to me.

By mid-morning, I was well enough to sit up. The man who had carried me to safety approached and sat down. He smelled of warm, earthy comfort and his skin glistened with a sheen of nut oil. It made me feel confident that he would care for me in the same way he cared for himself.

"Welcome. I am Bek. My wife, Su, is the one who bathed your face in our precious healing waters. I have many questions for you." He clasped his thick hands, placed them in his lap, and leaned forward. "But first, please tell me your name."

"I…" I choked because these were the first words I'd spoken in days. "My name is Ku."

The man smiled and nodded. "You look like you are close to my son's age. His name is Tsotem, or Tso. Perhaps when you are better, he can show you around our village."

I smiled. It felt so good to be around a man who was compassionate.

"You know," Bek said, putting his hand on my shoulder. "You are quite fortunate to have made it to us. No one has ever survived the desert."

I nodded. My chest felt charred, like it had been burnt from the inside. Indeed, I had come very close to dying.

Although I was grateful to be alive, some part of me was wary of these new people. "Where am I?"

"You are in an oasis," he continued, understanding that I knew very little of such a place. "An oasis is formed in a depression in the desert. Water tables below the earth feed our springs, wells, and trees, and nurture lush valleys to flourish. We are an island of water and flora within a sea of sand and we take pride in our waterfalls, high plateaus, therapeutic sulphur pools, and rich mineral springs."

"How did you find me?" It was hard to wrap my brain around such a place, where water was not only available but plentiful.

"We watch the buzzards around here, for clues of life. Wherever they are, there is either a live person or a person who has recently died."

Tsotem sat next to his father listening intently. He had a genuine smile, a prominent nose with a noticeable bump on the bridge, as well as a shock of flaxen hair that stuck straight up from a cowlick at the crown of his head.

Tsotem then said proudly, "I have very good eyesight and spied the buzzard in the distance. Rarely do buzzards come close to us, though, because…well, not many people make it through the scorching heat of the desert."

The sound of Tsotem's voice made me homesick for my family.

"And," he continued, oblivious to a tear that ran down my right cheek, "...we sat in silence watching the buzzard drawing closer until it got so close, we figured we would go investigate. That's when we found you. It was a miracle!"

Quickly wiping the errant tear, I felt dizzy and began swaying.

"For now, you should rest," Bek said, noticing my weariness. "We will leave you alone until tomorrow...or maybe the next day. Now lie down."

I followed his orders, but with one eye open to my surroundings. It brought tears to my eyes to experience such kindness from a stranger. My first priority, however, was protection. I thought of my father and his tenderness with my siblings and me.

Despite my vigilance, I slept better than I had slept in many years. And when I awoke, I found another flat stone plate; this time it displayed luscious fruit and was placed on the mat in front of me.

Su was clearing the sleeping area and came over to me when she saw me stir.

"You look so much better! Here," she said, delicately placing the stone plate laden with fruit into my hands. "This fruit will help you to gain strength."

I gobbled up the sweet yellowish fruit, which had been stripped of skin, and then moved on to a gorgeous, green, tart fruit with small white seeds. Su was right, I felt much better after eating them. In fact, I felt so good I sat up and tried to stand. When she saw this, she ran to my side and took my arm, as I was quite unsteady. *Why*, I wondered, *are these people being so kind?*

Walking wasn't so bad, but I saw that my feet were a mass of dry, cracked skin, which the blistering hot sand had caused during my desert journey. My legs had to get used to walking, but I managed to get the hang of things within a few minutes.

Tsotem approached us. He was flushed from helping his father hunt birds and small prey animals in the desert heat his flaxen cowlick bobbed as he ducked his shoulder underneath my arm and attempted to hoist me to my feet.

I reluctantly allowed him to support me as I took my first few recuperative steps. "I've never met a miracle before," he continued, "but my dad says you are one. How does it feel?" He took the opportunity of being close to me to do a thorough visual examination—scanning from my torso to my head and then straight down to my toes.

I defensively glared at him.

After checking out every inch, he concluded, "You look pretty normal to me. Although your legs are skinny and you've got huge feet. Maybe I'll call you twig legs."

I raised my eyebrows and murmured, "Bird beak."

And thus began our friendship.

Bek adopted me as his son and Tso made sure I felt welcome and "normal" wherever I went. There were about thirty people in the village, and only ten of them were children. I brought that number up to eleven.

Su and Bek enfolded me into their family and as I grew, they taught me the ways of their people, of the oasis, and of the desert.

Tso crafted boats and spoke of being surrounded by imaginary water instead of sand. We'd spend hours planning explorations beyond the desert, where we would seek treasure, adventure, and love. Our dream was to travel together and find new lands and new civilizations.

Over the next five years, Bek taught me about the element of water. I was educated in special divining techniques and irrigation. My defensiveness melted away and I came to call Tso "brother," Bek "papa," and Su "ma." But nothing completely removed my grief and my new family would watch helplessly as any kind of death (animals or people) would send me into hiding. These episodes would only last a day or two but my family felt at a loss as to how to help me.

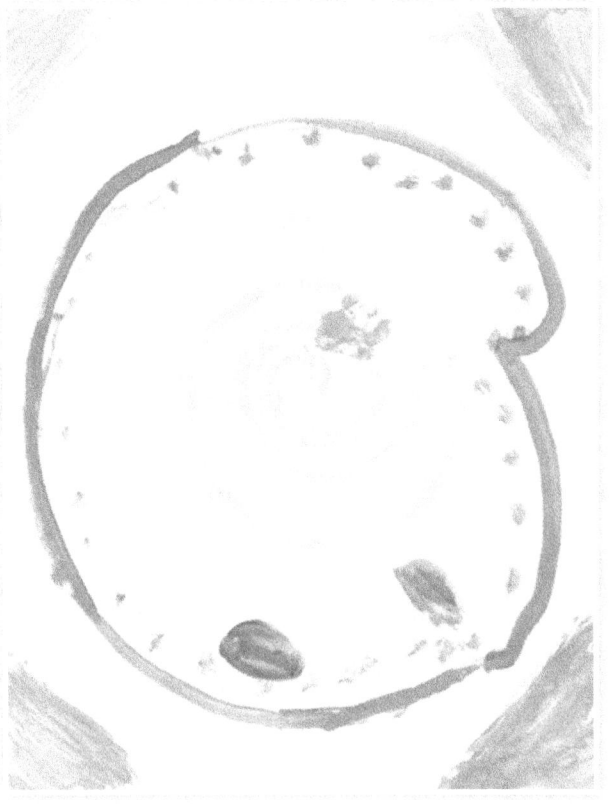

One day, Bek asked me to walk out to the far edge of the oasis. Silently, we looked out over the surrounding desert. Bek looked somber as he put his beefy arm around my shoulders and pointed out to the horizon.

"The healing you seek is beyond the confines of the desert, Ku."

"But Papa. I can't leave here. I love you all so much. Please don't send me away, please." I couldn't bear to hear words like this. It brought up the pain from the past as if it had just happened.

"There is a part of you that will never properly heal if it is not attended to. You have proven that you can travel in the desert and I will provide you with a map to the Temple of Karnack."

"But, Pa..."

"I have come to love you as my son, Ku, and because of that love, it would be wrong for me to keep you here."

We walked back to our family's shelter in silence. I went to my bags and pulled out Am's stone and held it in my palm. Am's words came back to me: "You can either let fear control you or let it go. The choice is up to you."

I fell asleep that night and dreamt that Am and Bek were discussing my future as I slept. I could hear everything they were saying, but I couldn't respond.

I awoke frustrated and angry and took it out on those closest to me—Su, Tsotem, and Bek. If one of them looked at me, I'd snarl and if they dared speak, I growled. Finally, Su told me to leave until I could behave civilly. So, I walked to the same area where Bek had delivered the news, which had so greatly upset me, and sat watching the desert world go by.

It was not scary anymore, the desert. Five years ago, when I looked out over the vastness, I saw a stagnant, des- iccated wasteland, unfit for human existence. But as I sat contemplating life, my fifteen year-old brain churning with thoughts, ideas, emotions—I saw the desert through new eyes. This desert was a beautiful place, one which defied human explanation and in which delicate, hearty ecosystems resided. I was filled with an intensely intimate love for this Earth and every being on it.

Then I heard the Call. It came from the south, carried on the hot breeze, and hit me squarely between the eyes. At first, the sound was only an erratic buzz. The more I breathed in the sizzling air and drew it deep within my soul, the buzz evened out to a spaced-out hum, then the hum became words. I jumped when I heard the voice. It was clear and located in the very center of my head. "I'm here." The voice was my childhood self—the one that the monster had imprisoned in the stone containing my healing gifts. "Never fear, Ku. I'm here."

CHAPTER XI

# Soul of Tso

## Ritual: Reciprocal Kindness
## Stone: Moonstone
## Blend: New Moon Elixir

---

*Write down eleven acts of kindness that other people have shown
you throughout your life. They can be minor—helping carry a
heavy item—or lifechanging—saving your life. At midnight
during a full moon stand outside with your list and ring a bell for
each item. Each time you ring the bell for an event say:*

*I fill my soul with appreciation.*

*Know that every time you send out appreciation for another soul,
your own is filled, too.*

*Blessed Be.*

"There has got to be some way we can use our gifts to escape." Hillary paces the length of the packed earth floor, then stops in front of Molly. "Do you get any kind of feeling about the woman who put us here?"

"I...uh," Molly puts her hand up to her forehead, then exhales loudly, "No." She frowns and looks over at the gorgeous baby napping in the carrier. "Except I think she is cruel and I don't like her one bit!"

Heidi says brightly, "I can see her. She is whispering into her cell phone, but I can't understand her."

"Well, turn it up!" Hillary says gruffly.

"I can turn it up all I want to. She's speaking in another language!" Heidi retorts.

"Oh." Hillary drops the gruffness. "Sorry."

"It's okay." Heidi kneels down and plays with the baby's toes. "What do you see?"

Hillary closes her eyes. "I just see her twirling a small pouch around on her finger. She looks pleased."

Molly speaks sharply. "She's not pleased. What you see is her masking the fact that she is extremely worried about us being here. We are threatening her livelihood. The key is in that pouch. Which doesn't really help us. There is a place where the grating has come loose from the frame but she doesn't think we'll figure that out." Molly massages her temples. "It feels like there is a vise on my temples."

A loud, wet farting noise comes from the carrier.

"Oh great! A baby with a wet and dirty diaper." Hillary huffs, turning to face Molly. "You couldn't have told us about the loose grate an hour ago?"

"An hour ago I didn't know I could pull information out of thin air!" Molly yells.

"Hey." Heidi has found the loose grating and it's big enough for her to put her hand through. "Stop arguing and help me! If I can put my hand in here, surely we can use something to pry it open."

"The pipe!" Hillary retrieves it and puts it through the weakened metal space.

Molly puts her hands on the pipe to help pry the grating away from the track. "Oh, no, we've got to get out of here."

"Why?" Heidi and Hillary also pull on the pipe.

"I'll tell you as we go," Molly says as the metal begins to give way. "Watch out, Heidi. Let's wiggle the pipe."

Hillary moves the baby carrier well out of the way of any harm while Molly uses a blanket to pull the grating with her hands. "Looks like someone hit this grate with the van."

With one huge crash, the grating gives way. Then a large piece of metal falls away, revealing a space large enough for them to escape. Molly grabs the baby carrier and they run for safety toward the adjoining tent's back area.

Once they are out of Heidi's earshot, Hillary whispers to Molly, "Why did we need to leave?"

"She just received a call saying that a baby is missing and she's on her way to come check."

"Thanks for saving us, Mol." Hillary says, squeezing through two stalls. "Follow me. Next on the agenda, changing that baby's diaper!"

On the other side of the market, Moa stares at the box, afraid to touch the contents—a silver piece with three parallel wavy lines.

"You can pick it up," Leti says, "it's yours."

"I don't understand. What does this have to do with the Statue of Ku?"

"There were two of these at one time. Hold the coin in your hands. You may be human now, but your memory is still intact. Perhaps it will offer you the answers you seek and you may find its mate."

Leti goes back to playing her rock game.

Moa moves into a pool of sunlight in the center of the rest area and examines the piece of silver. It isn't a coin. It is heavy and has three parallel wavy lines.

So much for the physical properties. Now, for the metaphysical properties. Moa pulls a small ottoman into a private spot and settles in, holding the piece in both hands.

Moa gulps for air. It feels as if she is being suffocated, but from within. Leti sees her and motions to her mother to help.

Together, they pry the coin from her hands. And Moa is able to finally pull enough air into her lungs.

"I'm going to call the medical team, just in case," Leti's mother says. "You need to be checked by a doctor."


Molly, Heidi, and Hillary ease their way back into the packed market via a series of circuitous narrow paths.

Hillary puts her hand up to her chest as she navigates through the masses. "Mol," she yells behind her, "you said Moa was near someone who cared for her."

"Yes." Molly and Heidi follow her down yet another crowded aisle crammed with people. Molly does her best to hold the baby carrier up to shoulder height so the baby is shielded from being knocked.

"I..." Hillary gasps and coughs. She is pushed aside by a man carrying a medical bag and a woman holding an oxygen tank. "Moa!" She sputters. "Can't breathe."

"Let's follow them. Heidi, hold on to the back of my shirt."

Molly tries to keep up but winces. "The vise in my head tells me that Moa is definitely the one they are here to help."

The emergency responders hurry through a narrow passage and into the rest area, the trio running behind them.

"Moa!" Hillary cries.

Molly and Heidi run to Moa's side. She smiles weakly and is lying on a blanket next to an ottoman and holds a small ornate box.

Hillary kisses Moa's forehead and holds her hand. "Oh, God. I missed you! Are you feeling okay?"

"I learned that I have a new gift. I experience other people's emotions as my own. The trouble is it almost killed me."

"We have gifts, too!" Heidi takes Moa's hand. "And look," she says, motioning to the gurgling baby in the carrier, his arms wiggling and legs pumping up and down. "I'm so glad you're okay, Moa."

Moa smiles and reaches her hand up to touch the baby's tiny foot, then says weakly, "I can't wait to hear the story of how you found him."

"Pardon me," Molly turns to Endo. "Does anyone have a diaper? This baby needs a change."

Endo nods and disappears.

"What's this?" Molly points to the small box in Moa's hand.

"I'm not sure." She gives the box to Hillary. "It is somehow connected to Ku. When I held it in my hand, I felt like I couldn't breathe."

Endo returns with a cloth diaper, pins, and several burp cloths. Molly nods gratefully and begins cleaning the squirming baby.

Hillary takes the silver piece in her hand, closes her eyes, and traces her fingers over the wavy lines. Suddenly, her body begins to shake uncontrollably and she throws the piece to the ground. "Well, I know why you couldn't breathe. The person who owned this coin was poisoned!"

I dashed back to our family area bursting with energy and news. It was time to go. On my way back I encountered Tso. He was bashing coconuts with a rock, and from the look of things had been at it for some time. Bits of coconut were everywhere, in his hair, on his face, and chunks surrounded him like a miniature village of people.

"Tso!" I yelled to him because he was still pounding as I approached.

He didn't look up but retorted, "Things were better without you, anyway."

"It's my destiny."

"What about our plans?"

"Plans?"

Upon hearing my last comment, he looked like he was about to explode. "Finding treasure, adventure. We were going to explore other civilizations together." My blank look sent him over the edge. He began bashing the larger bits of coconut, sending pulp flying everywhere.

"Those were just games! I can't believe you thought..." I caught myself from taunting him at such a delicate time and changed my tone. "Ma and Papa would be heartbroken if we both left."

Tso stopped pounding and looked at me—more like through me. "Don't use that pitiful tone with me."

"Fine, come!" I threw my arms up and walked away.

I could hear Tso slipping on his coconut shavings to catch up with me. Once he was at my side, his tone was vastly different. "We can leave tomorrow!"

He ran ahead of me to tell his parents and when I arrived—mere minutes behind Tso—Bek was bellowing.

"You are not meant to go, this is Ku's path. Not yours!" His normally soft features were red and taut and his thick hands were pressed into his temples.

"It is time, Papa. It is my dream to find adventure, treasure..." he tapered off, embarrassed as he heard himself.

"You sound like a child, but you are no longer one." Bek looked down at his son's stocky legs and feet. It was obvious that what he had to say was difficult. "Please think carefully about your choice to leave, Tso. Whether you leave or stay here, maturity comes from within." After a long silence he said, "It is your decision."

Su sat in the corner next to a painted clay bowl filled with purple berries and quietly wept. Bek slowly stepped over the bowl, sat down, and took her in his arms.

To allow them privacy, I walked to the opposite end of the oasis and surveyed the place from which I had come. It looked the same as the one where I would soon be headed, but it felt vastly different. When I thought of going back, I felt tightness in my chest. It was impossible for me to imagine doing so. As I faced the old desert, the Voice that had called my name earlier in the day did not exist. Five years had passed and I'd learned so much about myself since then. I said a silent farewell to that old direction and turned toward the new way.

I began to run toward the front side of the oasis, the one that faced my new adventure. It felt so free and open, and as I neared the very edge—where the lushness of the oasis met the dry sand—the calls came in loud and clear, "I'm here, Ku! I can't wait to see you!" It felt joyous, exciting, and terrifying all at the same time.

Tso spent the night away from us that evening and the following night as well. Bek helped me to prepare for my journey by supplying me with three indispensable tools: a stone hammer, a stone knife, and an axe. Su prepared her special delicacies: dates, olives, apricots, rice, and corn. Tso returned from his walkabout with the news that he was not coming with me. The two-day sabbatical seemed to change Tso. His mannerisms, intent, focus, everything about him was manlier. It was clear that this was his choice and no other person's.


The village held a feast in my honor. I was so touched by their kind words. The love and attention was so unlike anything I'd experienced in my life, it was difficult to absorb. Before my life in the oasis, leaving meant escaping, fleeing, and pain. This farewell was joyfully sad. Even though I would never see any of these people again and would miss them terribly, I felt pulled toward this new land—wherever it was.

The morning of my departure, I gave Su a warm hug and kissed her wet cheeks. Bek's embrace was so strong I thought I might lose consciousness. He pressed a gold coin into my hand and whispered tear-choked well-wishings in my ear. Tso's gift made me cry. It was an arrowhead that he'd found when he was five. When I'd first arrived in the oasis, he'd told me about how this was his good luck charm and it would never leave his hands. I sobbed as he peered at me through his lashes, his head lowered, a tear slipping down his chin.

I drank in my incredible family, these people who had taken me in as their own. I inhaled their generosity and gifts, breathed in the last of my home, and then exhaled as I strode toward my destiny.

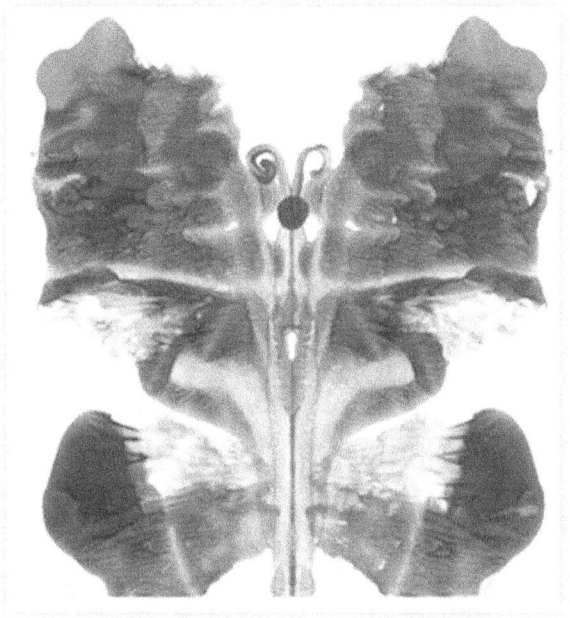

CHAPTER XII

# Unwrapping Gifts

Ritual: Inner Truth Serum
Stone: Lapis Lazuli
Blend: Sunrise Elixir

*Just before sunrise, create a nest of soft grass in a secluded spot in nature (or if you're inside, use blankets) and sit perched and ready to receive your truth.*

*As the first light of day appears, say the following:*
*I ask the light to bring my truth.*
*Repeat the incantation as the sun rises. Breathe in joy and anticipate happiness and peace.*

*Blessed Be.*

"Poisoned!" Heidi recoils from the group and stands up. "Who would do that to poor Ku?"

"Or maybe it wasn't Ku." Hillary says. "Was Ku human?"

"Yes, my mother came to me in a dream on the plane ride over and said, 'Some gods were human at one time. Ku was one of them.'" Moa expends her last bit of energy on these words and puts her head down on the pillow. Her face is pale.

The baby wiggles his arms and legs joyfully in his carrier.

"We need to get you back home," Molly says. "Excuse me." She speaks to the male attendant who is nimbly putting an oxygen tube below Moa's nostrils. "We'd like to take her back to the palace. Can you help us transport her to the market's entrance? We have a limousine waiting."

The attendant nods and picks Moa up, places a small canister of oxygen in her lap.

"Thank you for taking such good care of Moa, and also for the diaper." Molly smiles at Leti and Endo, then lifts the baby carrier up high, once again, out of the rest area and follows the attendant to the market's entrance.

Hillary turns to Endo and Leti, who have been standing at a respectful distance watching the foursome's reunion unfold and says, "Thank you both. You saved her life. We will all be forever grateful to you."

She and Heidi walk out of the tent and follow the attendant to the market's entrance.

Once they are safely traveling away from the market, Moa begins to perk up. She asks for some water and gulps it down as she props her feet up on the limousine's seat.

"Well, that was a bust," Molly says, placing the carrier between her feet on the limo's floor.

"What do you mean?" Moa asks between swigs.

"We didn't find the Statue of Ku." Molly grabs a bottle of water as well. "We need to find this baby some formula." She unfolds a clean white linen napkin from a polished wood cubby, dips it in the water bottle, and holds it up to the baby's mouth for him to suck on, but he turns his head.

"It wasn't a total waste, Mom." Heidi watches the dust fly behind them as the limo navigates the dry, rocky lane. "We found out that each of us has unique gifts. And Moa received a clue from her new friend. If anything, I'd say we are very close to finding Ku."

"Leti said that I've come to Egypt seeking more than a statue." Moa lays her head back on the soft leather cushion. "She's right. My mother came to me in a dream on the plane ride over and said that Ku's status as a god is in jeopardy."

"Okay, but how can four humans help a god to regain his divine status?" Molly asks.

"That sounds like a riddle." Heidi laughs then thinks for a moment. "By using our special gifts!" She bounces up and down on her seat. "Mom, remember how you were able to 'know' what was going on with the woman who caged us? Can you try that again?"

"Heidi, sweetheart. I was under stress. This is a completely different situation. I...wait..." Molly rubs her temples with both hands. "Ku's energy lives on within his lineage, which by now stretches across every continent to millions of people." She leans her head back on the seat and continues, "Without his soul connection, he risks disconnecting with those millions, and without his human connections, he will no longer have the ability to reach the celestial realm where all god energy exists. If that happens, millions of people will die. That includes Moa and her family!"

"She's right! That's exactly what my mother said to me in my dream." A flush returns to Moa's cheeks.

"Wow, Mol. For someone who just said the information you received when we were trapped was a onetime event, you pretty much nailed the Ku situation on the head." Hillary scoots closer to Molly. "Anything else?"

Molly appears to be searching inside her brain for any more information, then says, "No. That's it for now." She looks relieved and excited. "That was amazing. How did I know that?"

"That is called claircognizance." Moa nods. "It is the gift of knowing. There is also, clairaudience—hearing..."

"I have that!" Heidi smiles, "What is it called when you see things?"

"Clairvoyance," Moa says.

Hillary nods and looks out the window at the small mud huts and shacks, the dancing trails of laundry strung up between buildings. "It seems like you stumbled upon your own gift as well when you empathically experienced our emotions while we were trapped, Moa."

"Yes, clairsentience." Moa smiles. "It is odd to feel a gift like this in my human body."

"Did you have clairsentience when you were in human form the first time?" Molly asks.

"I didn't know what it was, but now that I look back, I think I probably did. One time my sister cut her left hand on my father's axe. I was with my mother delivering fabric, but I started crying and holding my left hand. I was inconsolable until I arrived home and saw my sister's injury."

Molly laughs. "Our little group seems to have every extrasensory power covered."

"Maybe the prince and his family already knew about our gifts and that is why they called for us." Hillary pulls her focus away from the dusty hills and mud huts zipping past.

"Now how on earth would they know?" Molly chuckles. "I can't imagine that they're psychic, too."

"I don't know. How did we discover our unique powers?" Hillary turns back to the view outside, "Well, if they don't know, the royal family is in for a little surprise because we now have the power to unlock whatever secrets they've been holding back from us."

The limousine's tires squeal as it turns in to the marble-paved driveway. Hillary, Molly, and Heidi aid Moa's exit. However, once she's out of the car, she makes a mad dash through the open front door.

"She's feeling better, I see," Hillary says to Molly as they watch Heidi mimic Moa's path.

Molly heaves the baby carrier out of the limousine and says to the gurgling infant, "You'll love this place, *keiki*! Lots to see here."

Moa does a baseball-type slide and lands directly at the feet of the prince and the king, who are deep in conversation. By the time Moa and Heidi get up, Hillary and Molly have reached them.

"Pardon us." Hillary stifles a laugh as she extends her hand toward the king. "Hello, I'm Hillary and this is Moa."

"Nice to meet you both." The king is a stout man dressed in a beige, linen tunic and pants. He leans over and extends a thick hand to Moa. "Hello, Moa. I've heard much about you."

Moa ignores the king's hand, and instead throws her arms around his neck and gives him a bear hug. "Nice to meet you!"

After the king recovers from Moa's surprise squeeze, he pats her shoulder and gives her a squeeze back. She holds on to him for five more seconds then quickly releases her arms. "Thanks!"

With a chuckle, the prince waves to a young male servant in a beige tunic and slacks waiting nearby. "I see you have a new addition. Unfortunately, I'll have to hear the story later. Please show the women to their rooms. If you'll excuse us, ladies, my father and I have some urgent business to discuss before dinner. Can we expect you this evening?" He directed this last part to Hillary.

"Yes," Hillary said with a wry smile. "We would love to attend dinner this evening. No room service will be necessary."

My journey in the desert this time was far different than the last. For one, I was older, stronger, and better prepared. I had also been sent off in a loving way and, therefore, could calmly plot my course and travel without worry. These things made all the difference. I had studied the stars while I was in the oasis and had been shown maps of a city where a large body of water stood, the Nile River. Due east was the Temple of Karnack. That was my destination.

The city, I was told, was inhabited by a brash and hearty people, and was ruled by a pharaoh. My skills as a navigator were strong and I had won many an endurance challenge with my peers. This journey would prove that my education had been worth the effort.

The pack I was given included my father's hunting sack, as well as Am's woven sack and her gleaming stone. I had created a nightly ritual in which I would hold the stone in my hand and imagine that it held all the powers I needed to survive in the world: protection, intelligence, physical strength, and compassion. Then I would hold the stone to my heart and imagine that these powers were within me, surrounding me and increasing daily.

It was lonely traveling by myself and, occasionally, I would talk with my father. During my previous trip I'd done so, but I'd all but stopped the practice when Bek became my surrogate father. He always had room for my stories about Father, and I loved him for this generosity.

My birth father, however, seemed to be a part of my soul. It was he who I turned to during my greatest challenges or when faced with my worst fears. Luckily, this trip offered very few troubles with weather. In fact, I moved quite swiftly, as if I was shepherded through the desert by angels whose job it was to deliver me unharmed to my destination.

The journey took me four weeks and noticeably absent was Apep, the buzzard, or any other creature of prey, for that matter. Except for a few curious lizards, I traveled alone. That is why, when I spied the first light of a fire—I'd arrived at night—I let out a whoop and hastened my pace. The excitement of human contact after such a long respite made my heart pound nearly out of my ears.

The faster I walked, the farther the firelight seemed to get, and exhausted from a full day's trek I opted to camp out before meeting anyone new. I reasoned that I'd be much better company with a good night's sleep and settled into my soft pad using my sack as a pillow.

BLAM!

I awoke on my feet, groggy but poised for battle. But all was silent. Then it sounded again and nearly knocked me off my feet. BLAM!

Shaking off the dreams that fogged my vision and mind, I finally located the source of the noise. An old man with long, gray hair was slamming a hammer into rocks just behind a large boulder. I had stumbled upon someone else's camping spot.

As I approached, the man stood up straight and wiped some sweat off of his brow. He wore a cloth around his waist, as I did, but his was made from a light-colored woven fabric. Touching my own fabric, a memory flashed through my mind. I remembered watching as Bek wove and pounded thin reeds that Tso and I had gathered from the base of a waterfall. Then he placed the mat in the sun to dry for a full week. After that he washed the entire mat in the creek until it became pliable and soft.

This man before me had loose skin, which hung off of his bones the way a woven rug does while drying on a tree limb.

"Would you like some help?" I asked.

The man looked at me warily. "Who are you?"

"I'm Ku."

"Well, Ku. You are on my property. I have purposefully created my home here so that I would not have to deal with any other people. Leave now before I have you arrested." The man returned to his task.

"Excuse me, sir, but could you tell if that is the Temple of Karnack below us?"

"Yes." He said without looking up. Then he ignored any further attempts I made to speak with him.

I gave up and went back to my bag. Surely there were kinder people in the city than this man. After all, if he had removed himself, it was for his own reasons. I packed up my belongings and headed down toward the city. From my spot on the hill, I had seen huts and a beautiful temple, which seemed to spring out of a beautiful lush valley. Now I could see more. The Nile's luscious sinewy banks, the sparkling center that curved and curled toward the horizon. I craved the tingling cool feel of water on my skin after three weeks in the desert.

CHAPTER XIII

Ritual: Soul Nourishment
Stone: Smoky Quartz
Blend: Pure Light Elixir

*Draw a circle on a piece of paper. Within the circle, write all the things you wish for, yearn for, and desire. On the outside of the circle write those people, things, feelings, patterns that keep you from attaining your wishes and dreams.*

*Envision that the items in the circle come to fruition before your very eyes. See each one play out, imagine that you've achieved your goals, and your dreams are set in motion. Upon completion, each accomplishment becomes a radiant light. Now imagine the circle glowing with the radiance and light of all of your accomplishments. Then see the light within the circle grow and overtake the items outside your circle. Imagine that your people, things, feelings, and patterns—your roadblocks to success—instead turn into light bridges. These bridges lead to accomplishments beyond your current desires.*

*You are meant for bigger things. Believe and it is so.*

*Blessed Be.*

"This is a strange request," Molly says, as she puts the baby carrier down on the central living area's velvet couch, "but, do you have any baby clothes around?"

"I think we'll be able to find a few pieces." The servant gives a wink. "Let me dig around and I'll be back."

Molly lifts the baby up out of the carrier. "Hey, Heidi, want to help me give this little guy a bath? He certainly needs one after our adventure today."

Orange and gold rays of late afternoon sunlight play off of the baby carrier and couch as Heidi heads toward her room. "I'm taking a hot shower and nap before dinner. How about you, Moa?"

"A shower sounds divine. Let's meet back here before dinner." Moa skips through her door, humming a made-up tune.

"Where do you think his mom and dad are?" Heidi cups a palm full of warm water in her hand and pours it over the baby's shoulder.

"I have no idea, love." Molly runs a clean white wash-cloth over his chest with one hand and supports his head with the other. He gurgles with delight and splashes his hands, sending water into his face. "Once we get him, and ourselves, cleaned up, we can ask the prince for help in locating the baby's parents. I'm sure they are frantic."

"What if they're dead?" Heidi doesn't look at her mother, but instead strokes the baby's head.

"Well, he would need to be adopted." Molly doesn't look at Heidi either.

"If I was his sister I would never let anyone take him away. That lady who took him, if she came back," Heidi, jumps to her feet, "I'd give her a karate chop!" She kicks the air with her feet, nearly missing Molly's head.

"Wow!" Molly avoids collision, soaps up the washcloth, and deftly cleans the baby's legs, genitals, arms. "You would be an amazing big sister! Can you please hand me a dry towel?"

While Molly rinses the wriggling baby, Heidi brings over the clean towel.

"Now, we'll put the towel here." Molly spreads it on the floor, lays the baby on it, and wraps him up, dabbing the water away.

When Molly and Heidi exit the bathroom, they see a woven basket loaded with onesies, diapers, wipes, blankets, a canister of infant formula, bottles, and nipples.

Molly unfolds a white onesie and lays the baby on the bed, turns to grab a diaper, and returns to an arcing stream of pee, which hits her left shoulder. "Aaaargh!" She grabs a receiving blanket from the basket and throws it over his privates in an attempt to stop the fountain.

Heidi doubles over with giggles. "Just like a fountain!"

Molly wipes off herself, the bedspread, and then the baby and quickly puts a diaper on him. "Well, that was a surprise. I've only heard of that happening."

"Did that ever happen with me?" Heidi watches curiously.

"Nope, this rarely happens with girls and it never happened when I was changing you."

"I want to take a bath, too. Can you help me run the tub, Mom?" Heidi heads into the bathroom.

"Sure." Molly snaps up the onesie and wraps the baby in a fluffy receiving blanket. She picks him up and says to him, "Now you get to help Heidi take a bath. Let's go."

While Heidi bathes herself, Molly pours a plastic cupful of infant formula into a bottle, pours in some bottled water, screws down the top and nipple, and shakes it up. "I'll bet you are hungry."

The baby smacks his lips and sucks as Molly positions him in her arms and settles on the bed, relaxing as he gulps down the formula. "Wow, you were hungry!"

When he is finished, Molly puts him up on her shoulder and pats his back until he lets out a tiny burp. She then lays him down beside her and snuggles him under the covers. Heidi towels off and joins them for a cozy nap.

Molly wakes at dusk, the purple, orange, and gold light creating glittering streams on Heidi's arms and on the lovely baby's cheeks.

At dinner, the conversation is lively and punctuated by the king's warm belly laugh. A servant cuddles and coos at the baby while the group dines on turkey, stuffing, and mashed potatoes. The prince stays quiet.

"You pried open the grate with your own hands?" the king asked Hillary.

"Yes." She laughs. "I never knew I had such strength."

"In honor of your safe return, we have prepared a traditional American Thanksgiving dinner."

"I love turkey!" Heidi stabs a piece of white meat with her fork.

Moa takes a huge bite and nods vigorously.

"We were hoping you might be able to help us find this child's parents," Hillary says.

The king and the prince exchange a wary look, then the king says, "We will do our best, but baby traffickers do a careful job of covering their tracks. Finding a child's parents in this situation is next to impossible."

Upon seeing their distraught faces, the prince hastily adds, "But we will do all we can."

"Thank you," Molly says, looking over at the baby.

After dinner, the group returns to their living area. Moa and Heidi talk animatedly about what they would do if Geti, the babynapper, returned. Heidi karate chops and Moa punches the air.

Hillary and Molly sit on the velvet couch, the carrier by Molly's side, and watch the girls with amusement.

Molly lifts the baby up and holds him up to her nose, takes a deep sniff, and lets out a satisfied, "Ahhhh."

Hillary seizes the chance, "Mol, you seem very comfy with that baby."

Molly smiles, "Steve and I talked about trying to have a boy."

"You sure have picked right back up with the baby care."

Heidi's and Moa's active play comes close and Molly suggests, "Why don't you move away from the baby?"

"We tried to have another child," Molly confides, "but I had a miscarriage."

"Oh, Mol," Hillary says, "When?"

"When Heidi was three." Molly looks over at the girls. "After it happened, I didn't get pregnant. We talked about adoption, but figured we'd wait and see."

The girls move, but the play migrates back and Molly's tone changes to a warning, "You are too close. Move back."

"This baby seems so comfortable with you. Would you consid…"

Suddenly, Heidi does a karate kick and clips the empty baby carrier, sending it flying. It lands on the floor with a crash.

"What did I tell you!" Molly says sharply.

Hillary jumps up to grab the carrier. The cover has come loose of the bottom, revealing an envelope with documents. "Hey, Mol." She brings the envelope over to Molly and opens it up.

Visibly shaken, Heidi scoots in next to Molly, "Sorry, Mom."

"It's okay, sweetie," Molly puts her free arm around Heidi. "I'm just glad the baby wasn't in it and that no one was hurt."

Moa peeks over Hillary's shoulder. "What does it say?"

"I don't know, I can't read Arabic. At least, I think that's what this is." Hillary looks at each page for any English words. "I don't see any words I recognize." She hands the documents to Molly.

"Let's find the prince," Molly says, rising. The baby is sleeping soundly. "I'd like to get to the bottom of this."

As alien as it was to be living in a city, I adapted quite quickly. The next man I encountered was a regal-looking man who was deep in thought, examining a large tablet with scratches and symbols on it. When I asked him a barrage of questions, he pointed toward a large stone structure with enormous pillars and statues on either side of the gaping entrance.

I stopped dead in my tracks. This temple reminded me of the place where my gifts had been stolen all those years ago. Suddenly, I was propelled back to the memory of that awful creature pulling out my very essence. When I walked inside, however, the place looked nothing like my vision. There were no stone stairways or hallways, only a wide space with an altar opposite the entrance.

There were flattened rocks for seats, and a wonderful smoky aroma wafted through the air. The place felt serene and my breathing began to calm.

"You seek healing?" A tall man with a kind face approached me. He was wearing a smooth linen cloth around his waist.

"Yes, I…" I searched for the exact words I needed, "I seem to have had something…uh…stolen and wish it to be returned."

"I am Gareb. And your name?"

"Ku."

"Follow me." He turned and walked toward the far end of the temple to an altar and a deep pool of water.

He sat on a marble slab and motioned for me to sit next to him. "You are lost." Even though he was sitting next to me, he seemed to drift off to a faraway place. His face changed. "We can heal you, but only you can regain your healing gifts by entering the Great Pyramid."

I was shocked to have this stranger speak with such familiarity about my gifts, but somehow I felt safe with him.

He seemed to come back from wherever he'd gone and shook if off with a shiver. "I'm not sure what that meant. Can you enlighten me?"

Before I knew what was happening, the entire story poured out—my stolen gifts, my family's slaughter, desert travails, and eventual rescue by Bek and Su. Through it all, Gareb sat calmly nodding. It felt healing to speak the words, and the more I spoke, the more restored I felt.

When I was finished, Gareb dipped his hand into the pool, then placed his hand on my heart and proclaimed, "I anoint the warrior Ku and ask for healing."

Slowly, I let the tears come. Then I began to sob.

"You began your journey when you entered the first temple as a child and the second temple as a young man. This is your third stop on your journey to healing."

Gareb rose and escorted me back to the temple's entrance. "You have three more temples to visit before you can enter the Great Pyramid and regain your gifts. Follow the path north to Dendra. Safe journey, Ku."

Even though if felt as if we'd been speaking for only a few minutes, it had grown dark outside. I turned to thank Gareb, but he was gone. Something made me walk back to the spot where we'd been talking; the pool into which Gareb had dipped his hand and anointed me, mere minutes ago, was empty and completely dry.

As I headed north in the dark toward Dendra, fear began to well up inside my chest. *What if the healing I completed in Karnack wasn't real?* If fear was my burden, it seemed that Gareb had been able to provide relief. No matter. I was determined to regain my healing gifts and avenge the monster who stole them. I chose to camp at an overlook just above the temple so that I could be first to enter the next morning.

I awoke to the chirping of birds and was amazed to see a line beginning to form at the Dendra Temple entrance. Quickly packing up, I gingerly stepped down the steep embankment to the temple entrance and took my place in line.

A gentle young woman with braided hair and a lovely white sheath dress was in front of me. Her face was pleasant and I couldn't imagine how she needed healing.

"You look healthy." As I attempted to make conversation, I shifted my pack awkwardly and nodded at her.

She kept on smiling and turned back toward the entrance without a word.

Well, two could play at that game. If she didn't speak, then I wouldn't either. I watched in frustration as other people filled in the line behind me and began chattering away. Soon a vendor approached us carrying round fist-sized knots of bread.

The milky nape of the young woman's neck distracted me as I spoke with the vendor. The woman shook her head and I decided against the bread, even though I was famished. I had no money to spend on such things and had packed enough sustenance for a month.

When the woman's turn came to enter the temple, I watched with curiosity as she ascended the marble steps and walked through the vast pillar-lined portal. What wondrous healing could Dendra offer? But before I could think any further, it was my turn.

Unlike the Temple of Karnack, the Dendra Temple contained small seating areas where various healers sat and spoke with hushed tones. As my eyes adjusted to the light, a slight woman with light-brown hair and soft, blue eyes motioned to me. I sat down in front of her and she took my hands in hers.

"Love is yours, but you must first sacrifice your ego." The woman spoke succinctly.

"What's an ego?" I asked.

"Pride keeps you from truly allowing love to enter your heart. Until you give up your pride and relinquish your ego, you will never know love."

The woman looked past me toward the entrance and motioned to the next person.

"Wait!" I protested. "I don't understand."

"Your turn is up," the woman said calmly. "If you wish to gain more insight you must wait until tomorrow."

I reluctantly rose and heaved my pack upon my back as the next person, a puffy woman who smelled of roasted manure, shoved her way into my seat.

Outside, my eyes readjusted to the light and I saw her on the temple steps, hunched over. She was the young girl from the line, crying uncontrollably. Her name was Hueneme and she said she had not spoken a word since her mother died. That was when she was twelve and now she was eighteen.

"But you're speaking now…" I loved her mouth. The way she formed her words and the gentle sound of her vowels made me want to hold her.

"Yes. I…" she began to cry again and wiped her face on her sheath dress.

Finally, she was able to speak and told me of her father's death when she was six, and about her mother's subsequent death when she was eight. Hueneme had been left to serve the pharaoh's mother and after she died, Hueneme sought healing from the temple.

"So, are you happy that your voice is back?" I couldn't imagine leaving her side.

"Yes." She brightened up and her breathing returned to normal. "There is someone I fear and that is why I came here for healing. His name is Rhamanak and he is going to ask for my hand in marriage. I had no need for my voice until I realized I don't want to marry him, and my voice is the only thing that will allow me to protest his advances. I was hoping to get information about another man who might marry me instead, but the woman inside the temple was no help at all.

Listening to her silken voice, I realized I never wanted to leave her side.

"Rhamanak followed me here," Hueneme whispered, motioning to a lanky man with a scruffy beard and a permanent sneer, who was watching us.

Feeling rash, I asked, "Do you trust me?" and to my amazement, Hueneme nodded. I asked her to accompany me to the Saqqara Temple and she agreed. Traveling with her slowed me up, but I didn't mind one bit.

Her gentle lilting voice reminded me of the brooks in the oasis and her laugh... well, it made me forget all my worries and fears.

We arrived at Saqqara late in the afternoon and she entered the temple with me. A wrinkled old woman hobbled up to us and gave us a slip of papyrus with the mark of Thoth on it. "You will need this to pass through the gates of the Great Pyramid."

She pointed to a cavernous well in the center of the temple in which we were to call our ancestors to us. Hueneme went first and called to her mother, her father, and the pharaoh's mother, with whom she had become close.

I called the names of my family: Am, Bek, Su, and Tso. I asked that they bring back my healing gifts encasing my trapped childhood.

The woman nodded and closed the iron gates of the temple behind us, and we ventured out into the early evening dusk. Our last stop before the Great Pyramid was the Sphinx. We decided to camp just outside the town near a small stream. I caught a few small *coti* fish and she gathered some edible flowers and grasses. We dined that evening beneath the stars and I fell into a joyful slumber.

As the sun rose over the Sphinx, I tiptoed to a bluff and saw the purple and orange colors move across the feet and face of this glorious temple. When Hueneme finally rose, we collected our things and made our way toward the entrance.

The Sphinx healing temple was crowded inside, and Hueneme and I squeezed in and attempted to find a spot to sit. We finally settled in an area just large enough for both of us to sit cross-legged and meditate. The minute I closed my eyes, I could tell that something was different. The air had changed, and it felt as if all people, sounds, and the floor had instantly fallen away and I became suspended in midair. When I opened my eyes, Hueneme was at my side with her eyes closed and all was the same, but the minute I closed them, I was back in a suspended state.

As I relaxed in to the feeling of floating in midair, a humming sound vibrated around my head and neck. Soon I was lifted to the ceiling and propelled through the roof. I was shown the picture of the planet and constellation to which this temple corresponded. A voice gently told me that I was connected with the giant planet, Jupiter.

Then I was slowly placed back into my body and when I opened my eyes, I was back in the same place I was before.

Hueneme and I had great fun relaying the stories about our meditation experiences as we exited the Sphinx and searched for a camp in the evening.

"Don't you have somewhere you need to go?" I asked Hueneme as we hiked up through the brush and around a craggy rock formation.

"I'm exactly where I need to be," she said with a smile.

My heart melted and fear sliced it in half. Love inter-twined in my heart with grief and became an entirely different feeling—leaden and clingy. She deserved more than my version of love.

I wondered aloud why, after all these healing experiences, I could experience these feelings even more intensely.

"Healing does not take away our feelings, it reconnects us to humanity. When we are more connected to our humanity, we are more equipped to handle intense feelings." Hueneme seemed to glide through life and take in the world like one would breathe air, in steady, consistent doses.

But when the time came, fear stopped me from entering the Great Pyramid.

"What If I came all this way and now it's too late?" I ruminated.

"You can either let fear control you or let it go. The choice is up to you." Hueneme spoke the exact words that Am had said to me that night before I left Fet's farm!

Then, I heard the Voice call to me—the very one that called to me from the desert—"Please," it said, "please don't let fear keep you from reclaiming me and our healing gifts."

I told Hueneme about Am, showing her the stone that she'd given me. Hueneme held the beautiful stone up to the light. Then she stood and took my hand and pulled me toward the Great Pyramid. I shoved the shimmering gem back into my pack, took a deep breath, and entered the small doorway.

The air was still as we walked through the first of many narrow passageways. Hueneme never let go of my hand, even as it became awkward to maneuver through the twists and turns in the tunnels. We came to an opening and decided to stop and meditate, just as we'd done in the Sphinx.

This time, I closed my eyes and found myself speeding through a tunnel of light. No matter how hard I tried, I could not open my eyes. I arrived, with a plop, somewhere else. The surface was powdery and the air was dusty. Just before I screamed in terror, Hueneme appeared right next to me. A feeling of warmth and safety overcame me and I saw my healing gifts hovering above me. I could hear a child's voice, my voice from childhood.

"You are healed when you believe you are whole," the voice said. It seemed as if a long lost piece of me was finally coming home, and I opened my arms wide to welcome the child with an embrace.

"Thank you for not giving up," the child said.

"I love you," I said to the beautiful, bright-eyed boy.

Outside of the temple, I grabbed Hueneme and we began to dance. I was giddy with my healing gifts and the full return of my inner child. "Did you receive anything in the pyramid?" I asked her.

During our short journey together I had grown to love Hueneme more than anyone I'd ever known.

She gave me a secret smile, then said quietly, "That's for another time. For now, I honor your newly acquired abilities."

"Let's celebrate with a treat!" I announced, and traded a small bracelet of woven *bendali* leaves—highly prized gifts from the oasis—for two large knots of bread. I set my fist-sized crusty bread on my bag, held Hueneme's hands, and spun her in a circle. Hueneme held her bread in her hand as we laughed and sang. I felt as rich as a king and as blessed as a god.

We kept on dancing, and a crowd gathered around, clapping until we finally collapsed next to my bags. I reached for the bread and gobbled it down, appreciative of this small feast.

The minute I had licked the last bit of crust from my lip, I felt the tingle on my tongue. My vision blurred and I doubled over with stomach pains.

Hueneme held me in her arms as a shadow fell over us. A smirking Rhamanak stood above us.

By the end of the evening, my stomach was empty, and I began to vomit blood.

Hueneme wiped my forehead and rinsed my mouth with clear water and searched for a *ka* receptacle. Egyptians believed that when someone was ill, they could put a person's soul, or *ka*, into a statue for safekeeping until they were healed, at which time the *ka* would be returned. If the person died, the statue would be buried in the tomb along-side the mummified body.

"*Hem om na ka*," Huneme whispered into my ear. "I will keep your soul safe, Ku. You are not alone." A tear rolled down her cheek as she attempted to keep me comfort-able. My head pounded as she cradled it in her soft lap and scanned the area for a suitable statue in which to place my *ka*, but none could be found.

The female vendor who sold the bread went in search of a statue and Hueneme thanked her for the help.

"*Hem o na. Se ku ka*," my beloved continued to incant—as I wandered in and out of consciousness. "These are magical words to transmute all soul properties and abilities from the physical body to an object."

I began to cough and struggle for breath, and Hueneme placed her cheek on my forehead. "Please don't leave, my love. Please…" My chest rattled and she placed her hand there and exhaled. "While we were in the pyramid, an angel brought a child to me and placed it in my arms. She said that it was our unborn child. He's inside me now and wants to meet you, Ku. Please don't leave us."

A gust of wind blew the flap of my sack. Hueneme deftly unearthed Am's stone and repeated the words to transmute the soul properties.

My last breath was caught in the stone. Hueneme sobbed as she held my soul in the palm of her hand. A crowd had gathered at my feet

"Se Ku Re," she quietly intoned, "light your journey home." Then she felt a hand on her shoulder and looked up to see the bread vendor with a *ka* statue, but she was too late.

Several large men hefted my lifeless body over their heads and carried me to a public burial area. This is where paupers with no family were laid to rest.

The rest of the story is simple. The pharaoh took Hueneme into service as his fourth wife's hand servant. Her work at the pharaoh's palace ensured the continued care for Hueneme and our son—she had indeed conceived our child through the incandescent power of the Great Pyramid. Hueneme kept Am's stone—containing my soul—safe throughout her lifetime. When our son died, however, he was placed in a modest tomb that was raided and the contents were scattered and sold throughout the kingdom. Priceless gemstones were placed on reed mats in dusty street markets, gold jewelry was traded in dark alleys for scraps of food, and even Am's stone was tossed into a grab bag of semiprecious stones for children.

The story of my death at the base of the Great Pyramid spread throughout Egypt and I became a local hero. Hueneme kept alive the story of how I received my healing abilities, and then dying immediately, and I became a source of inspiration and continued faith for those who sought their own healing abilities.

This is how I became known as the god Ku.

# CHAPTER XIV

# The Hammock

### Ritual: Peace
### Stone: River Rock
### Blend: Simple Elixir

---

*Take a smooth river rock in your right hand. Picture a
troubling circumstance in your mind's eye and then
exhale your troubles into the stone. Imagine that
the river rock absorbs your troubles.
When you are through, toss the rock into moving water (a creek or
the ocean works well). As you throw the rock, say:*

*Peace is in me and surrounds me.
I am Peace.*

*Blessed Be.*

"The child's parents are dead." The prince leafs through the documents discovered from the baby carrier. "Apparently, this child was gained legally because there are no heirs to care for him."

"Who is he?" Molly looks over his shoulder, looking for answers.

"Adem Muhamet" the prince reads. "His parents died in an auto accident outside of Cairo and he was put into an orphanage. The question is how the woman you met was able to take him and the other babies. My father and I will make sure this woman is found. Justice will be swift, I promise you."

"What happens to the…um, Adem," Heidi asks.

"He will be put back in the orphanage." The prince shrugs.

"Oh, we can't let that happen! Mom, we have to do something. What if he is taken again?" Heidi bounces next to Molly.

Molly looks at the baby, then at Heidi. "Heidi, why don't you go back to our room with Moa. Hil, do you mind going with them?"

Hillary gives Molly's shoulder a pat and she heads back to the room with the girls.

Molly yells after them, "No karate kicks!"

"Aw, Mom," Heidi says.

"I don't know what the laws are," Molly says, looking into the prince's eyes. "Our agreement was that you would pay for our house if we helped you find the statue. I know we haven't found it yet, but is there any way that you would consider adding the adoption of this baby?"

The prince smiles for the first time since Molly returned from the market. "I'll see what I can do."

Molly waltzes down the hall with little Adem dozing on her shoulder. When she arrives in her room, she places him in the bassinette that sits close to the bed and snuggles next to Heidi, who is already asleep.

The next morning, Molly awakens to the luscious smell of bacon and eggs outside her room. Heidi is already up and playing with Moa in the living area. The baby is awake and coos when he sees her. "Hello! Let's have some breakfast." She picks him up and says, "Uh oh, you need a change."

A servant has kindly prepared a bottle of formula. Molly makes a plate of fruit and eggs for herself and Heidi. Then she nibbles as she gives Adem his bottle.

Heidi and Moa play dress up with Hillary's clothes as Molly and Hillary sip coffee and the baby lolls on a receiving blanket on the floor. He seems mesmerized by the rainbows created by the morning light hitting the prisms on a chandelier.

"I can't imagine what Adem has been through." Molly looks down at the smiling infant. "It looks like he has something...oh my gosh, I think it's a brand...on his hip."

"You're kidding me!" Hillary kneels down next to Adem. "Which side?"

Molly joins her and pulls the left side of the diaper down to reveal the raised bit of skin.

"Oh! Who on earth would do that to a baby?" Hillary touches the raised, discolored patch of skin.

"I know," Molly says.

Hillary gets a faraway look, then recovers. "I saw the strangest thing just now. In my mind's eye, I saw a tribe of people performing a ritual. They all had this scar."

Molly shudders. "I'm not letting him out of my sight. Not even for a second."

"Are you going to try to adopt him?"

"Yes. The prince said he'd help facilitate the process if we help him find the statue." Molly rises and pours herself another cup of coffee.

"Which we haven't even come close to doing," Hillary says.

Moa emerges from the bedroom out of breath from a game of tag, with Heidi on her heels. "Hey, Molly." Moa plops down next to Adem's head. "Heidi says the baby has a cool scar. Can I see?"

As Molly peels back the diaper, Moa lets out a squeal. "That's just like my coin!"

She speeds out of the room and is quickly back. She holds the silver piece, which Leti gave her in the market, next to the baby's scar.

"They do both have the three wavy lines," Molly says warily.

"Leti said, 'This is what I came to Egypt for....' I thought she meant the piece of silver, but maybe she meant the baby."

"I'm lost." Molly sighs.

"This baby is a sign." Moa gets a faraway look. "Blessed light. He is 'the Healer.'"

"Okay. Now I'm lost, too." Heidi declares.

"I think she's...um...I don't know what the word is...I think she's channeling," Hillary whispers.

Moa's gaze remains detached and eerily connected to an unknown source. She continues, "This child will forevermore be called 'Ku Re,' the divine luminous Light from within, and will bring wealth and healing to all he encounters. Subsequent generations will bear the mark of the chosen one. I anoint you the Prince of Light, Lord of Healing, blessed god, Ku."

"Do you think the baby is related to Ku?" Hillary whoops, "Imagine if we asked for a statue and instead got a flesh and blood ancestor. Amazing!"

"But how do we prove it?" Molly touches Adem's silky hair. "His papers say he's Adem and from…well, I guess we can't trace his parents. They're dead, so they can't lead us anywhere."

"Well," Hillary dims only slightly, "at least we're in the right place. If anyone can find the answer, it is the prince."

Molly looks at her sister carefully, noting with interest the pink in her cheeks.

Later, in the royal library, the prince shakes his head as he leafs through another set of legal documents. "It looks as if these people were ordinary citizens. Adem's mother was an only child who came from a working-class family. Adem's grandmother was a teacher and his grandfather was an auto mechanic, and they passed away when Adem's mother was a teenager. Adem's paternal grandmother died during childbirth having her third child, and the paternal grandfather was forced to put Adem's father as well as his brothers and sisters in an orphanage. Adem's father was the only survivor when a fire killed his siblings."

Heidi and Moa are off playing with a female servant as Molly and Hillary take turns holding Adem, who seems unusually fussy.

"It's hard to imagine the tragedy that family saw. Sadly, it seems that Adem has no living relatives." Hillary picks up Adem's birth certificate and scans it for information as Molly jiggles the baby in an effort to calm him.

"From what my assistant found, it looks as if he is the last of his lineage." The prince rises. "Now, if you'll excuse me, I have some pressing business." With a perfunctory nod, he exits.

"He's been so moody," Hillary says, looking around the room. "He's hiding information, I just know it." She walks over to the computer and sits down.

"It's almost like he's got a family secret of his own." Molly stops jiggling and stands behind Hillary. "See anything?"

"You know, I had the strangest dream last night," Hillary says absently as she clicks on various files. "Good thing the prince didn't log out."

"What was the dream about?" Molly sits on an ottoman behind Hillary and places Adem up on her shoulder.

"An older woman with an incurable illness was calling for her son and husband…" Hillary begins.

"Only they were in the room with her," Molly finishes.

"Did she have a blue nightgown with…"

"Red roses embroidered along the color." Again Molly finishes Hillary's sentence. "And on the nightstand was a potted…"

"…purple orchid." Both Hillary and Molly speak these final words together.

"Wild," Molly says. "Let's get Heidi and Moa, I'm ready for lunch."


The prince and the king arrive late to lunch. Molly, Hillary, Heidi, and Moa are chatting up a storm while Adem squeals and squawks in the arms of a loving female nurse in a white tunic and pants.

"I really want to swing in that hammock!" Moa squirms in her seat as a black-clad male server dishes out fresh fish and vegetables onto her plate. "Want to come with me after lunch, Heidi?"

"Sure!" Heidi proudly displays her manners by nodding a silent 'thank you' as the server places a dollop of béarnaise sauce onto her plate.

When the prince and the king finally settle into their seats, Moa has already dug into her meal. "When," she puts a huge forkful of poached salmon into her mouth, "will we get to meet the queen?"

"Moa, that's not polite!" Heidi counters.

"But, I figured she hasn't been around…" Moa starts.

"The queen is away on holiday," the king says gruffly. "Never you mind."

Moa gets a determined look, "I think you're lying."

A shocked silence falls on the table until Molly clears her throat, "Ah, hmmm…Moa, Heidi is correct. If the king says the queen is on holiday…"

"She is not!" Moa yells. "I know she's here. I had a dream that there's a lady who is very, very sick and she needs Adem's help."

"I think it's time that we leave." Hillary grabs Moa's arm and pulls her to her feet, quickly escorting her out of the room.

"She's here!" Moa protests. "She's in bed with a blue nightgown with red roses along the collar and…"

Hillary, stunned by the coincidental dream, releases Moa's arm. Standing just inside the door, Moa continues to babble and massages her bicep, "and she had purple orchids on the bedside table."

This time, everyone stops eating and gapes at Moa. The prince's and the king's faces are both ashen. The silence is finally broken when Heidi accidentally knocks a spoon onto the floor, which lands with a loud CLANG.

After what seems like an interminable silence, the prince motions to the female servant. "Granti, will you excuse us?" His voice is hushed and raspy. "You can give the child to Molly. Thank you."

The king is incapable of speaking and sits with his eyes downcast as the prince waits.

Then, when the room is clear, he speaks. "Moa, Hillary, please come back and sit down. It is time we were honest with you. You must understand that this is being told to you in the strictest of confidences."

A chorus of commentary erupts from the group. "Of course, yes, we won't tell a soul."

The prince continues. "Moa, you are correct. The queen is gravely ill. She and my father tried for years to conceive another child to no avail. Although she kept her troubles to herself, I know it must have been very difficult for her. I can't imagine the pressure she must have felt. When I was young, a doctor promised to help her conceive a child, but instead he gave her a drug that shut down her entire reproductive system. It was a grave accident, and although he apologized, the damage was done. From then on, she consulted specialists to reawaken her womb. Finally, an herbalist promised that he had the answer to my mother's prayers. The herbs, however, did serious harm to her body and she fell into a coma. She has been unconscious ever since you all came. Now, we fear she might be close to dying. Just before lunch, my father and I met with a specialist—the latest in a long line of many who have examined my mother—who said he could not help her.

"The reason we guard our secret so closely is that our family's reign is in jeopardy. There is a group that wishes to wipe any royal blood from the country's soil and has wished so for thousands of years. They are the descendants of Rhamanak, the man who murdered Ku. The group, the Rindodala, thought they might help to restore order in our government by bringing back our ancient artifacts. However, the Statue of Ku has gone missing. So, you see, this struggle has been going on for generations, and my mother's existence keeps our lineage in power. Needless to say, we are at a loss." The prince trails off.

The grief-laden silence is cut by a sharp, high-pitched tone. The light in the room changes to a pale green. Each person in the group is mesmerized, held in place until the tone abruptly ceases.

"Well," the king says, breaking the silence. "That was odd. Although, I must say, I do feel slightly better."

"It felt like we went somewhere," Heidi says brightly, "and then came back."

"I saw three images." The prince still has a faraway look. "First my mother in bed, then a crystal labyrinth, and last, a medallion with three wavy lines on it."

"Pardon me," the king speaks slowly. "But it sounds as if you speak of the mark of the Healer. I read of this as a child but thought it was a myth."

Molly digs her fingers under Adem's onesie and pulls the diaper up to reveal the unusual scar. "Is this what you heard about?"

The prince leaps up. "We must take Adem to my mother's side!" He takes Molly's arm and ushers her as she holds the baby tightly; they all move quickly out of the dining room.

Inside the queen's chambers all is still. Light pours from two paneled French doors leading to her bedroom, and a somber female nurse opens the door as the group silently files in one by one, surrounding the queen's bed.

Although she is deathly ill and unconscious, Queen Pheah somehow radiates a serene dignity. Her bed table is laden with numerous pill bottles, droppers, and a crystal water pitcher. She does not stir. The prince looks at Adem, then to his mother and back to Adem.

"Something's missing," the prince sighs. "Don't you feel it?"

Molly shrugs. Hillary shakes her head and Heidi and Moa stare, transfixed by the unmistakable elegance that this beautiful queen possesses.

"The statue!" Hillary announces in a hushed voice. "Didn't you say that your nephew was retrieving it in an attempt to regain order in your kingdom? Perhaps that's what we need."

"Perhaps." The prince wilts. "But after years and years of searching, we thought we finally had it only to have it lost when it hit Egyptian soil."

The group ponders the prince's last words in silence.

"You know what?" Moa continues to gaze at the queen. "I want to go swing in that hammock. Come on, Heidi."

CHAPTER XV

# The Light of the Beholder

## Ritual: Portal of Light
## Stone: Amber
## Blend: Light Elixir

*Portals are energetic doors into new ways of thinking and existing. During your lifetime you will cross through Time Portals (becoming a teenager or an adult are two examples), Maturity Portals (when you learn life lessons) or Belief System Portals (when you break learned patterns). There are portals that you can create yourself, and this ritual is meant to allow you to access a place of Light in your world.*

*Find a space indoors where you can remain undisturbed for at least an hour. Spray the Light Elixir around your ritual area and light a single white candle (any kind will do).*

*Sit cross-legged and put your hands in prayer position at your heart. See yourself, in your mind's eye, walking along a path of light. You are surrounded by a starless, cloudless night sky. As you walk, you feel the light warming your feet and pulling you forward. In the distance, you see an arch and you instantly feel connected to the Light.*

*The closer you get, the more connected you feel. When you finally arrive at the arch, you feel an intense love coming from the other side.*

*If you pass under this arch and into the Light, you will be filled with love, warmth, harmony, health, healing, and happiness.*

*In this space, all of your emotional needs will be met, all of your worries are taken care of; you are healed, whole, and supported in every way.*

*If you feel any fear about walking through to the Light, allow the Light to dissolve those fears (same thing for any other emotions that arise—anger, sadness, anxiety...). When you are ready, walk into the Light.*

*Know that you can stay here as long as you wish, and if you find yourself back in the darkness, you may return.*

*Blessed Be.*

"**E**nough with the hammock! You've been obsessing about that ever since we got here." Hillary attempts to stop Moa by throwing her arm out, but Moa dodges around and hooks Heidi by the arm, dragging her out into the garden.

Molly shakes her head and moves toward the garden. "This is ridiculous. Newly human or not, that girl has got to learn some manners."

Hillary follows behind Molly to back up her sister and, with nothing tangible to do in the queen's chamber, the prince and the king wander out to the garden, as well.

Outside, the dry air swirls around the group. Everyone stands awkwardly, anticipating a certain confrontation. Heidi faces them all as she and Moa silently swing higher and higher. Moa looks toward the garden.

"Young lady," Molly storms up to the hammock and puts her foot on it to stop the swinging. "Turn around and look at me."

Moa, however, stays put with a stony stare toward the mystical garden as Molly ramps up for a lecture. "We are guests in someone else's home. The next time an adult asks you a question, you look him in the eye...."

There is no doubt that Moa is far away and is absolutely ignoring Molly. Nevertheless, Molly continues as Moa scoots off the hammock and walks idly toward the statues.

"Of all the insolent," Molly stomps toward Moa ready to continue the diatribe, but Moa squeezes in between the obelisks, out of Molly's reach. Kneeling, Moa disappears from view.

"You can sit there as long as you want. We can wait here all day," Hillary yells around Molly. Heidi has slipped off of the hammock and now cowers behind Hillary, wanting no part of the action.

"Can you believe this?" Hillary says indignantly to no one in particular.

"Our journey has taken us across the ocean..." Moa resurfaces from her hiding place with a huge grin. "...through crowded markets, and beyond our own levels of personal comfort. These are treks, stretches, and leaps. But what if the statue..."

Molly squints, trying to figure out what exactly Moa is up to, and the rest of the group shifts uncomfortably on their feet.

The sun makes the fountains sparkle and the lush grass glitter. Moa holds up a moss-covered statue and says, "What if the illusive Ku has been with us the entire time?

"Oh, my Lord!" Molly cries. "Is that the actual Statue of Ku?"

"Incredible!" The prince rushes forward to examine it as does Hillary, the king, and Heidi.

"Look, three wavy lines on the side of the statue, just like Adem!" Heidi rubs her hands along the statue's side.

"Thank you, Moa." The prince gives a bow and takes the statue in his hands. "I believe this may be the final piece in the puzzle to healing my mother."

This time, Molly, Hillary, Moa, and Heidi follow the prince.

Heidi pulls Moa aside before they enter the queen's chamber for the second time. "Moa, this is your family's statue! Are you going to just let him have it?"

Moa nods and then says solemnly, "Yes, you are right, Heidi. But I believe this is the right thing to do." She continues walking to the bed.

"Didn't your mother say it would save your whole family?" Heidi is incredulous.

"Sometimes you must heal the present in order to heal the past," Moa says with an enigmatic shrug.

"Mother." The prince's voice shakes. "I believe this is yours." He places the Statue of Ku on the bed at his mother's side.

Again, nothing happens.

"Oh, come on!" For the first time, the prince shows his true emotions. "You've got to be kidding!" He pounds his fist against the bed, which shakes violently. "Wake up!"

The king speaks up. "Son, there are some things that are not meant to be. Perhaps it is time we accept defeat."

"NO!" the prince screams, "I will do no such thing! After tracing the statue back to Moa's family, finding her, bringing her here...I was sure my mother would be healed."

Molly, Hillary, Heidi, the king, and Moa take a step back as the prince unravels. He hits at a small table, knocking it over with a loud clatter, while books, the queen's medications, and Hillary's purse scatter on the floor. The contents of Hillary's handbag leave a pagan trail of essential oil and paper from her diary. Her wand escapes its folded fabric enclosure, hits the base of an EKG trolley, and shatters into shards. From the depths of the green leather purse, an opalescent stone bounces out and ricochets off of a gilded dresser, landing unbroken, at the prince's feet. He reaches down in fury to fling the offending stone out the door but Hillary yells, "STOP!"

"This will not bring your mother's health back," Hillary says gently as the prince begins to sob. "I know you are frustrated. I am so sorry."

She steps close to him and gathers his large shoulders in her arms, embracing him tightly. He reciprocates the hug and his crying subsides.

As he recovers, Moa scoots over and touches the prince's hand. He relinquishes the stone to her small hand and gives her a sad shrug.

Moa walks around the room holding the stone up to the light, looking through it as if it's a spyglass through which she may view unseen wonders Finally she reaches the queen's bedside where light is pouring from a nearby window. She holds the opalescent stone up to the light and smiles as colorful rays of pink, green, and yellow dance about the room and over the queen's face.

Moa picks up the Statue of Ku and places the stone in an indentation of the statue's belly. It fits perfectly.

This seemingly insignificant stone, the one Hillary found on her first visit to Thomas Square Park, risking a lifetime of curses and bad luck as she removed it from Honolulu, is Am's stone.

An unearthly light shoots from the statue and lands on everyone in the room. Adem's little body radiates a beautiful golden hue and the queen opens her eyes. Her face glows with an eerie blush, as do her hands. She silently swings her legs to the floor and stands ready to embrace her husband and son, who rush to her side.

The light transforms everything it hits. Hillary, Heidi, Molly, and Moa are each filled with healing white light, which cradles every cell of their bodies. The queen's chamber is transformed, the walls are replaced by pure light, and a sparkling crystalline labyrinth replaces the ceiling.

The group watches in awe as I, Ku, exit the labyrinth. My appearance is clear, yet filmy, vibrant, and opaque. Grateful to finally be free from my maze of imprisonment, I acknowledge each one of my benefactors with a jewel, which corresponds to their extrasensory gift.

"Petalite," I send a beautiful glittering light yellow stone into Heidi, "to enhance and protect your clairaudience."

"Opal," I say as a gleaming white opal appears in Hillary's hands, "for your intuitive third eye and brilliant mind."

"Malachite," Molly beams as a gorgeous green stone materializes in her hands. "May you enjoy increased discernment."

"Each of you has brought me here with your unwavering faith and power." I energetically connect their jewels together and continue, "If it was not for you, I would not be here. Thank you."

As I take a step out of the labyrinth, a bulbous gnarled monster with putrid yellow ooze pouring from what appear to be eyes and a mouth bubbles up from the floor in a thick opaque pool of ooze. He growls, "You do not deserve to move forward. I am more worthy and capable than you of honoring the true nature of the Healer. Accept defeat, Ku, just as you did in the sacred temple, or you and your lineage will be annihilated."

I extend my arm toward the queen's bed and send an energetic tether, which wraps around my long-sought statue, and draw it directly into my being. As I receive the newly activated statue, my energetic body changes colors—red, orange, yellow, green, blue, indigo, and finally white. "After you stole my gifts, I felt ashamed at being a 'mere mortal,' and wandered the earth with every intention of reclaiming my precious healing gifts and seeking vengeance. You preyed upon a child's innocence and took advantage of my desire to help. There is no honor in your actions."

The queen, prince, and king recoil from the stench that emanates from the monster's yellow, pus-filled boils. "I will live wherever fear exists and that is everywhere. My strength was fed by Fet, the Anuenue, and Rhamanak. Each of these humans feared your strength and few remaining gifts, and I was able to channel their fear, to hurt and—eventually through Rhamanak—kill you." The monster sends a fiery orange blast toward Ku.

The queen's chamber suddenly morphs into the temple basement from long ago. The group recoils as the stone walls, the floor, and the heavy wooden door transport the room to that fateful moment when my gifts were stolen. But I am no longer a child.

"Power does not exist with human gifts or abilities. It resides within a human's soul and is strengthened though adversity. I mourned the loss of my gifts for a large part of my life but eventually realized that I am as powerful as I believe I am. When I understood that, I understood true power. My strength and protection come from those who believed in me, but I must first believe in myself. The stone which Hillary so carefully protected and Moa used to activate my statue was the one that Am gave me long ago." As the monster's blast hits me, the energetic hatred magically activates the three stones I have given to Hillary, Heidi and Molly and transforms into a large fiery ball of white healing light which hits the monster like a nuclear blast.

Screeching, high-pitched tones reverberate around the chamber and the monster bubbles and melts, finally transforming into a silver pool. The pool dissolves and a shimmering diamond floats above the space where the monster once stood.

As I approach the diamond, I intone, "I willingly receive my healing gifts once again, and this time I promise to share them only with those who are able to fully receive them." The diamond shimmers with newly infused energy and moves directly into my heart.

After this proclamation, I approach the queen, who stands with the support of her husband and son.

"You have suffered greatly in an attempt to honor your lives with another child." Then I place my hands on her lower belly and send radiant pink and gold healing light into her womb. The queen's drawn face is transformed and her cheeks glow. "This is my gift to you, a blessed child."

The queen gasps with ecstasy and places her hands on her belly. The prince and the king hold her close, grateful for the dream come true.

A shaft of light appears from above and I step into its shimmering rays. This ray of light extends to the center of the room and a faint outline of a light-filled doorway materializes.

"Ku! What about Moa!" Much to everyone's surprise, Heidi speaks up.

All eyes turn to the sweet little girl who holds Moa's hand firmly. Heidi continues, "She hasn't asked for anything." Moa keeps a steady gaze at her own feet. "She helped save me, my mom, Hillary, and even Hawaii. She became human, for goodness sake! Not only that, she gave the prince her mother's statue of you so that you could heal his mother!"

I exit the light shaft. "Moa. Would you like to come with me?" I motion to Moa, who reluctantly looks at Heidi and then back to me. Slowly, she releases Heidi's hand and cautiously walks toward me.

"Will I see my family?" she asks.

"Yes, Moa. You will."

With a smile, Moa takes my hand and we step into the light shaft and transform into the light traveling upward out of view. Just before we fade away, Moa gives a jubilant wave to the humans who love her most.

## CHAPTER XVI

# Going Home

### Ritual: Healing the Hearth
### Stone: Moonstone
### Blend: Grounding Elixir

---

*Fill a cup up to the rim with earth. At midnight on the first day of the month (can be any month), hold the cup up to the starry night sky in offering and say:*

*Wherever I am is home.*
*I will no longer run.*
*Wherever I exist is home.*

*Blow all your fears into the cup of earth. Imagine the dirt cleansing and clearing your body of its ability to put down roots. Putting down roots sometimes means travel and other times it means staying put. Know that you can choose where your home is at any time.*

*Blessed Be.*

Hillary, Heidi, and Molly lose consciousness from the astral residue G-forces of our Light departure. The king, queen, and prince, however, are unaffected.

The prince helps Heidi and Molly up.

"I feel dizzy," says Hillary. "That is the residual effect from Ku's and Moa's departure," the queen says kindly as she helps Hillary to her feet. "Did you hit your head?"

"I'm okay." Hillary looks shaken, too, and notices that the queen's chamber has returned to its regular state.

"I didn't mean that Ku should take Moa away." Heidi tears up and Molly gives her a squeeze.

"Maybe it is for the best," Hillary reasons, trying her best to hold back her own tears. "After all, Moa did sacrifice her immortality. Now, hopefully, Ku will reunite her with her family and she will finally get what she needs."

"But what if we're what she needs?" Heidi sniffles.

Molly holds the sleeping baby, Adem, close to her face and reaches her free arm around Heidi to pull her close.

"I'm going to miss her, too." Hillary tears up.

"You needn't worry about Moa," the queen says, seated in a rocking chair next to her bed. "She is accessible."

"What exactly does that mean?" Molly bristles as she rocks Adem in a tufted recliner. "We will miss having her around."

"I understand that you feel pain at her absence," the queen says reassuringly. "But you will soon be reunited."

Heidi brightens, "You mean she's coming back?"

"Let me explain." The queen takes her husband's and son's hands,

"Just a minute!" Molly interrupts. "What you're going to say is that Moa is 'with us in spirit.' We lost a husband…a father…" Molly is shaking with fury. "Nothing upsets me more than when I hear someone say that I can talk and the person who's gone 'will listen.' They might be able to see and hear me, but I cannot see them. It is lonely to talk and never get a response! LONELY!"

The queen continues compassionately, "You may not be able to see them with your eyes, but you can see them with your heart. And in your heart, that person's soul essence will be immortal. You'll be able to access them whenever you desire."

"But I *can't* see them—or feel them. Heidi and I had a brief, beautiful, angelic moment with my husband, Steve, and now he's gone. I will not have our hopes raised."

Molly struggles to get up and leave, but she has difficulty because she has Adem in her arms and is holding back the tears.

The queen does her best to stop her. "Things are different now. I promise, I promise."

"How can you say that? We worked so hard to find the statue for Moa and, in the end it seems it helped everyone but her."

"Oh, no. Moa got what she needed."

"How do we know? All we have is your opinion. She could be anywhere…" Molly trails off, hovering near the queen and on the verge of exiting.

"Then she isn't coming back?" Heidi squirms next to her mother.

Molly takes Heidi's hand, "Come on, sweetheart." Mother and daughter walk hand in hand toward their rooms.

"You may not realize this," the queen calls to them, "but as the Statue of Ku was activated, we were all transformed.

Although you are still fully human, your gifts—you know, the ones that you discovered while searching for Moa—have been…" She searches for the word… "enhanced."

As the group leaves, the prince calls to Hillary.

When she approaches, he takes both her hands in his and bows his head. "Thank you for showing such strength, Hillary. You have remarkable strength and wisdom beyond your years."

Hillary sees something in the prince's eyes that she never noticed. It looks as if an extra color has been added to his irises. She gives his hands a squeeze as she departs.

When Hillary arrives back in her room, Molly is hastily packing and calls out to Heidi, "Make sure you grab all your things."

"You can't be serious…" Hillary chuckles at Molly's ire. "Mol, I know we've experienced some odd circumstances, but, we're all okay. Let's stay and enjoy Egypt…"

Molly is visibly irked as she continues to gather belongings for herself, Heidi, and Adem. "You feel free to stay, Hil. But, we're getting out of here. Whatever just happened in there with the queen, they got what they needed." Molly slams her suitcase closed and zips it up. "They got the Statue of Ku, the queen is healed, they're a family again…and, I'm not an expert, but Egypt hasn't had a reigning royal family in at least sixty years. So, who exactly are these people anyway."

Heidi runs into the bedroom, her suitcase bumping her heels, "Okay, Mom. I'm ready."

After a beat, Molly picks up the baby carrier in one hand, her purse and suitcase in the other, and says, "Hil, if you're not coming, that's fine, but I'm taking Heidi and Adem and we're going home."

"But," Hillary tries to catch up to Molly, "what about Moa?"

"Yeah, Mom." Heidi's little legs move quickly and her suitcase bumps her heels. "We have to find Moa. How are we going to do that?"

The group is now in the atrium and headed for the foyer where they first encountered one another.

Molly doesn't slow. She gets to the door before Heidi and sets Adem's carrier down to pull open the heavy front door. "For now, I'm focusing on the safety of my children and myself. As for you…" she picks up the carrier and follows Heidi out the door into the dry afternoon air, "you are an adult and can do whatever you wish."

Molly and Heidi continue down the marble walkway lined with statues, with Hillary in tow, and Molly mutters, "I don't care how much money these people offered me…"

"Mol, how are you going to get home? Hillary pleads. "You don't have any money."

"Mom?" Heidi huffs as she stumbles over her feet.

"Keep going, sweetie." Molly is out of breath, too. "We're almost to the road."

"You're going to the airport and then what?" Hillary is angry now. "You have no money. No money means no plane ticket…"

"Mom!" Heidi yells.

The group is beyond the entrance now and Molly sets the baby carrier down and turns around to look her sister in the eye. "I will figure it out! Haven't I always? What the…" Molly is speechless.

Hillary turns around to face the palace and lets out a scream.

"Mom, where did the palace go?" Heidi quietly.

The palace has been replaced by the Great Pyramid. Hillary spins around.

"What...where's...the palace," Molly stammers.

"We're at the base of the Great Pyramid." Heidi says mystified. "How is that possible?"

The hot wind blows Heidi's suitcase over. Hillary leans over to pick it up and sees a bus, with a cloud of dust billowing from behind. It pulls up about ten yards away and tourists begin disembarking. They look weary, bored, and hot.

"Let's ask for help." Molly, obviously disoriented, wanders over to a distracted-looking middle-aged mother wearing blue Bermuda shorts and a pink golf shirt, who is fanning herself. "Pardon me," Molly says.

The woman ignores Molly completely and yanks her teenage son by the arm and shrieks, "We came all this way to see the Great Pyramid and you are going inside!"

The boy hangs his head sullenly and lopes toward the yawning base.

Molly tries another tourist. She approaches a young male. He wears plaid shorts, a tank top, and leather sandals, and is picking his finger nails. "Excuse me." Molly tries to be polite. "I wonder if you could tell us where we are?" The man walks right by her without even acknowledging her existence.

"Well, of all the nerve." Hillary shakes her head. "Um, sir," she approaches the bus driver. "Would you mind telling us..." The bus driver doesn't even look in Hillary's direction. "Sir. SIR!" Hillary is frustrated and puts her hand on the driver's shoulder to get his attention, but it goes directly through him!

"Oh, my Lord!" Hillary jumps back. "Molly." What exactly happened to us?"

"I'm scared." Heidi stands close to her mother. "What is happening?"

Two teen boys roughhouse and run toward Adem's carrier. "Wait," Molly calls and rushes to snatch the carrier away from being kicked. But one snickering boy makes it to the carrier before she does and he runs directly through it. It's as if the carrier doesn't even exist.

Molly touches Hillary's shoulder. "Well, *we're* here. I mean, we can touch, see, and hear each other."

"Let's walk around the pyramid and see if there is any evidence of the palace," Heidi says, "Or at least where the palace was before it uh...disappeared. Maybe we'll find something."

"Good idea, Heidi." Molly takes her hand and Hillary follows them around the corner to the opposite side. When they reach the far end of the base of the pyramid, Heidi squeals, "Look!"

The woman see the rocky ruins of the Japanese garden and run to the rocky dusty remains.

"This was where the Japanese garden and brook were. That means that our balcony was up there." Molly points in the general direction of where it may have been. "It's hard to imagine nothing is left. Not even a shard of broken pottery."

Heidi calls out from behind a small pile of rocks. "I think I found something. "Hillary and Molly struggle with the baby carrier as they navigate the rocks and slippery sand. They both laugh, though, when they see the iron Shinto statue. It is weathered, but intact and definitely recognizable.

"We're at Great Pyramid and have found this iron...I don't know, is it a sculpture? I'm sure it means something, but I have no idea." Molly sighs.

"I do!" Heidi's tone brightens. "I'll be right back." She scurries around rocks and disappears back around the corner of the pyramid.

Molly looks at Adem, who has slept peacefully through the entire ordeal. "This baby can sleep through anything!"

She reappears with her backpack. "I have something that might help us." She unzips her bag and pulls out the ancient book from the glass bookcase in Hillary's room.

"Heidi, this book is not yours to take!" Molly chastises her daughter.

"Well, it might be the only way for us to figure out what happened..." Hillary takes the book and Heidi turns the pages until she comes to a picture of the iron statue that sits in front of them.

"Wow, this is handwritten. I can't read it, Aunt Hillary, can you?"

Hillary squints, then reads aloud:

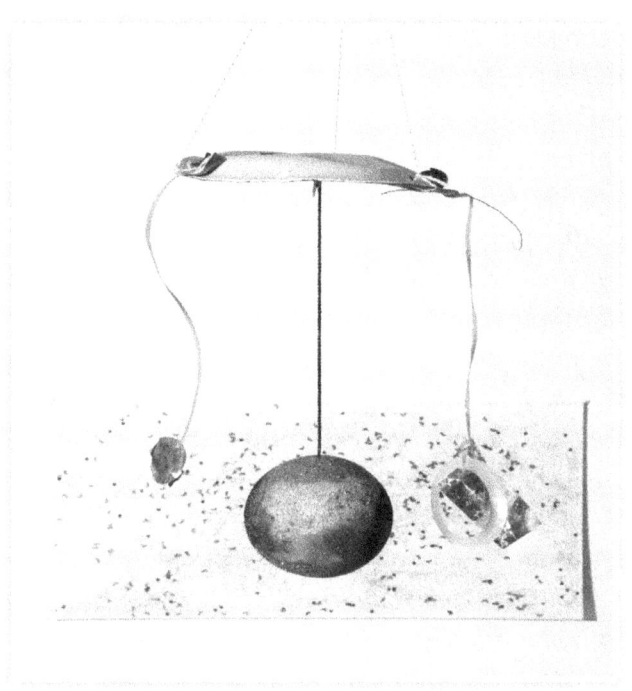

The Prince of Jupiter

It has been said that gods ruled as kings before Earth was formed, and celestial sovereigns were bound by an oath to their planetary realm. The people who said this, however, never met the Prince of Jupiter, who single-handedly transported the inhabitants of Jupiter beyond their meager planetary confines to a world where desires were manifested with a thought and dreams were a three-dimensional reality. It was all because of a glorious, mystical accident.

The prince was obsessed with the afterlife and spent every waking moment studying what happens at the moment of death. He learned that the physical body contains two distinct ethereal bodies, the 'Ba' and 'Ka.' The 'Ba' or soul leaves the body at the moment of death and returns to a collective group of souls where it will reincarnate into another body. The 'Ka' departs the body but stays nearby. It remains a psychic imprint or "spirit" which can roam freely but *remains detached. It was the 'Ka' body that fascinated the prince the most. The 'Ka' can make journeys to heaven, hell or can relive its human life for eternity.*

*The prince wondered what happened to the 'Ka' while the body was still alive. His curiosity led him to a meditation practice in which he attempted to send his own 'Ka' on "errands." He became quite adept at allowing his 'Ka' out for short excursions and equally skillful at calling it back into his physical body.*

*As the prince continued his unorthodox self-guided education, the queen, who had fallen ill shortly after the prince was born, spent much time in bed, which left the burden of raising and caring for the prince to the king. Despite the stressful family arrangement, the king dedicated himself to giving the increasingly overcrowded planet of Jupiter some much-needed elbow room. The king's initial exploratory missions found a suitable planet called Earth. Although the atmosphere was not ideal, the royal metaphysicists had created alchemical conveyance structures, pyramids, which would allow any Jupiterian to materialize on any planet and to calibrate to the atmosphere.*

*The first exploratory excursions to Earth found locations for three conveyance structures. Metaphysicists also calculated that one year on Jupiter equaled one hundred years on Earth. Construction began when the prince was a baby and concluded when he was fifteen. The aim was to link other pyramid conveyance structures—PCSs—with energetic vortices on the planet Earth and constellations beyond Jupiter's galaxy. Each PCS included two transportation areas: The King's Chamber and the Queen's Chamber.*

"The Queen's Chamber!" Heidi says. "That's where all the healing took place while we were in the palace."

Hillary continues reading:

*What no one could have planned, however, was how the PCSs would react with the intensely powerful, naturally occurring healing vortices on Earth and the prince's 'Ka' exercises. The young prince begged his father to be part of the first test group for the newly erected pyramids.*

*When his father refused, the prince sent his 'Ka' body into PCS where it successfully rematerialized on Earth! Although his 'Ka' was separated from his physical body, on Earth, the prince experienced all sensations on earth as if he had a physical body. As he exited the main portal into Earth's atmosphere, he accidentally cut his hand on a sharp crystal at the mouth of the pyramid. Wrapping his hand in his cloak, he continued on his adventure. The prince explored the lush foliage and crystal-blue waters, which flowed nearby. He dipped his hand into the lake to test the temperature and his cut healed immediately!*

*Upon his return and after he reintegrated his 'Ka' into his physical body, the Prince was punished for his disobedience. He promised he would never attempt to travel through a PCS or release his 'Ka' again. Meanwhile, the PCS project fell out of fashion. Most Jupiterians, it turned out, would rather not travel through the PCSs but favored their newly developed astro vehicles instead. So the project was abandoned.*

*By the time the prince was twenty, he fascination with using the portals turned to a full obsession. Based on his own healing experience with the beautiful crystal lake, he wondered if a PCS could access the incredible healing powers of Earth for his mother and he, once again, begged his father to go back.*

*His father, however, was not pleased that his son disobeyed him, and the prince snuck into the healing chamber.*

*Legend says that the prince convinced his father to allow him to separate each of their 'Ka' bodies, including his mother—now, gravely ill—and they would go, as a family, through the portal for healing. When they arrived on Earth, however, they found that all the lakes and foliage had turned to desert. Sadly, when the family tried to return to Jupiter, the PCS failed. They remained suspended on Earth in stasis. Their 'Ka' bodies were all they had, as the family built a virtual kingdom. That is, until they were discovered by the Anuenue. These* entities were the bridge to the other world. The Anuenue told them that their PCS had been overtaken by the Egyptians—who could not see or hear the royal family because of their vibrational state—and the PCS was renamed the Great Pyramid. Egyptians believed the pyramid was constructed by pharoahs as a burial tomb. The only chance of rescuing the family from imprisonment was a powerful statue in honor of a young man who died at the base of the pyramid. The Legendary Ku was the only human in Earth history whose 'Ka' and 'Ba' were transferred directly into the statue where they remained intact. The Anuenue said that they would find the statue and, through Earth inhabitants, find a way to free the royal family from eternal imprisonment. The group of benevolent Earth women chosen for this task was given guidance through Moa, a mystic guide. What the Anuenue did not tell the royal family was that the statue alone could not help them; instead, they needed a special stone to activate the statue and thus heal the queen. Moa placed the stone into the statue to release the royal family from their stasis.

While the royal family was on Earth, they tried several times, in vain, to return home through other PCSs on Earth. Their final attempt at escaping through an Earth vortex in Japan was thwarted by an evil force, which came in the form of a spindly limbed crone. This evil force was nourished by the stolen gifts.

With the Anuenue's help, the king imprisoned the evil crone in a stone temple, which he embedded in the forests of Egypt.

She remained there until a young Ku freed her from her confines where she fled to the island of Japan. His good deed bound them together for the remainder of Ku's Earth life and eventually caused his demise.

The king felt that the PCS from Japan—called the iron Shinto—was safer with him than in the hands of such an evil force, so he shrank it and transported it to his virtual palace for safekeeping.

Molly shivers despite the intense heat. "Where are our bodies?"

"I think the reason those tourists couldn't see us is because these are our 'Ka' bodies have separated from our physical…uh oh…" Hillary gives an ominous look toward the Great Pyramid's stone entrance. "What if the 'evil force' that Ku defeated somehow transported our physical bodies to Japan?"

"What would make you think that?" Molly tries to steady her breathing. She is terrified of what the answer might be.

"If the evil force has a 'Ka' body perhaps it went back to Japan to…"

Molly interrupts Hillary, "If? And how would we get there celestial helicopter?"

"Mom," Heidi pipes up. "We have our very own portal right here."

"I'm not going back in that Pyramid." Molly stubbornly says. "God only knows what might happen once we're in there."

"No." Heidi points to the iron Shinto. "Didn't the book say that the iron Shinto was a portal?"

"She's right." Hillary smiles. "We could try…"

"No, I think we should stay here." Molly is adamant.

"There is an incantation." Hillary scans the text. "It says that we can place our hands on the shrine's roof and…"

"The stones that Ku gave us can help." Heidi says proudly. "Mom. Do you have yours?"

"We are not going anywhere!" Molly grumbles.

"We are invisible, Mol!" Hillary raises her voice "And we have to find our bodies."

"We don't even know that our bodies are in Japan." Molly protests, but Hillary and Heidi smile at her.

"We have to start somewhere." Hillary says.

"Let me see that…" Molly takes the book out of Hillary's hands. After Molly has read over the text, she shakes her head and sighs. "I feel like I'm going crazy. If it wasn't for you two, being invisible along with me, I don't know what I'd do. Come here, Heidi." She embraces her daughter, cradles her in her arms and gazes over at the carrier holding Adem, who is sleeping peacefully.

"Mom." Heidi takes her mother's hand and gives it a squeeze. "Look at the iron Shinto!"

They all turn to see a flickering light within the iron Shinto.

"Well, if that's not a sign, then I don't know what is." Hillary walks toward the small metal structure and kneels down. "A light in the middle of nowhere."

Hillary stands up, digs her hand into her pocket and holds out her gorgeous white opal. "I'm going to Japan. Who's with me?"

"I am!" Heidi's yellow Petalite shimmers in her tiny outstretched hand. "Maybe we'll see Moa."

Molly slowly gets up, her Malachite in her right hand and she picks up Adem in his baby carrier with her left. She takes one last look up at the enormous pyramid in front of them before placing the carrier on the Shinto's roof.

"Okay, *keikis*." Molly strokes Heidi's soft brown mane. "Let's go."

An unearthly mist gathers around the group as they brace themselves for the journey ahead.


End

Discover other books in the Moa Series:

**_Moa_**

**_The Iron Shinto_**

# About the Author

Tricia Stewart Shiu is an award-winning, screen-writer, author and playwright, but her passion lies in creating mystical stories. Her latest series, The Moa Books, which includes Moa, The Statue of Ku and The Iron Shinto, were, by far her favorite to write.

Learn More about Moa
Facebook:
http://www.facebook.com/MoaBook
Website:
http://www.Moa-Book.com
Moa Blog:
http://tstewartshiu.wordpress.com
Follow Tricia Stewart Shiu on Twitter:
@tstewartshiu

www.ingramcontent.com/pod-product-compliance
Lightning Source LLC
Chambersburg PA
CBHW072132170626
46813CB00004BA/1540